Tide Turning
A Langley Calhoun Mystery

by

Lars R. Trodson

Mainly Murder Press, LLC
PO Box 290586
Wethersfield, CT 06129-0586
www.mainlymurderpress.com

Mainly Murder Press

Copy Editor: Jack Ryan
Executive Editor: Judith K. Ivie
Cover Designer: Mike Gillis

Copyright © 2014 by Lars R. Trodson
Paperback ISBN 978-0-9895804-9-6
Ebook ISBN 978-0-9887816-7-2

Published in the United States of America

Mainly Murder Press
PO Box 290586
Wethersfield, CT 06129-0586
www.MainlyMurderPress.com

Dedicated to my parents

~

Acknowledgments

Very rarely can any creative endeavor be accomplished without the help of others, and this novel is no exception. I have to thank Amy Wallace, Matt Stewart, Nicole Andrews, Chip Noon, Cresta Smith and Judy Levine for their direct involvement in the preparation of this manuscript. There is also the indirect involvement of many more — Ron Reilly, Clint Wynne, Joe Cooney, Debbi Tillar, Rob Ciandella, among them — who offered their encouragement almost on a daily basis throughout the writing of this book. This kind of enthusiasm and support is essential for any writer. I am, as always, grateful for that and their friendship.

One

Thursday, February 28, 3:00 p.m., Ed Lustig's law office, Manchester, NH. The worst thing a man can hear is the sound of another man screaming.

That's what Langley Calhoun heard coming from Ed Lustig's office down the hall. It was a scream, a screech, a yell. Men are not supposed to cry out like that.

Langley ran down the short hall, carrying his phone. He thought Ed was having a heart attack. When he turned the corner into the office, Ed was lying on his back, on the floor behind the desk.

Langley leaned over Ed and punched 911. Then Lustig said, clear as a bell, "Get me up."

Langley put the phone to his ear.

"Get me up. I'm all right."

Langley put his hand on Ed's chest to keep him down. "I want to …"

"Hang up," said Ed.

Langley said into the phone, "White male … "

"Hang up." Ed stretched out his arm as though he expected Langley to lift him up.

Langley looked at his friend. He cradled the phone between his ear and shoulder and lifted Ed up. "Hold on," he said into the phone.

Lustig stood, steadied himself, brushed himself off. He grabbed the phone away from Langley, ended the call and handed the phone back. He gave Langley a slightly embarrassed glance and started looking around the office as though he had lost something.

"Ed," said Langley. "Ed!"

Lustig looked at Langley. "What?" he said, a little peevish.

It was perfectly conceivable, given how much Ed Lustig drank and smoked and how overweight he was, that he would have a heart attack at the age of fifty-seven. Langley had worked for Ed Lustig as a private investigator for the past few years, and they were more than co-workers now, they were friends.

"Are you okay?"

"My phone," said Lustig.

"What?" said Langley

"I lost my phone." The color was returning to Ed's face. "It went flying."

"Are you okay?" said Langley. He found himself unnerved at the thought of something happening to Ed. He was enamored of Ed's lusty approach to life. He even kind of respected it, but it was a fantasy that could not last. Langley knew that, and he was reminded of it now.

"I fell asleep with my phone on my chest," said Lustig. "I have it on vibrate. The phone buzzed when it was lying right here." He tapped his sternum. "When the vibrating started it woke me up, and I thought I was having a heart attack." He looked under his desk. "So I fell on the floor," he said and started to laugh. Ed pointedly did not say that he had screamed. "No big deal. Go back to your office."

"Ed."

"I'm fine," Lustig said. "Thank you, my friend, thank you." He was still breathing pretty hard.

Langley patted Ed on the shoulder. "You're sure?" he said.

"Yes. I'm fine."

"Ed."

"Langley," he said with some annoyance.

Langley went back down to the hall to his office, and before he was even in his chair he smelled cigarette smoke wafting down the hallway.

Two

Same day, 3:30 p.m. Langley had just started to open a letter from his brother Brian. The letter had a return address of the Federal Correctional Institution in Littleton, Colorado. Brian had been incarcerated there for the past fourteen months, and he was due to be released at the end of the year.

Langley had been running his thumb underneath the sealed flap when he had heard Lustig scream. Now he picked up the letter again, tore it open and began to read.

"I used to call you Barrabas." That was how the letter began: "I used to call you Barrabas.

What was this going to be, Langley wondered. He looked at the rain hitting his window. It was a cold, gray day, and Langley looked at the puddles in the street, and he heard the whoosh of the cars as they pushed through the pouring rain.

"I used to call you Barrabas."

Resentment. Vindictiveness. Those two emotions characterized, in fact were, Langley's and Brian's relationship.

Langley looked at his brother's handwriting, which was so familiar, and couldn't get past the first line. Barrabas. It was what Brian had called Langley after their brother Danny died. Danny fell out of a tree when he was twelve, and Brian, Danny's twin, always blamed Langley. Brian revered Danny and so, when the death of Danny was still hot and tormenting, Brian used to call out to Langley, "Hey, Barrabas."

It was simple and elegant. Barrabas. The unworthy one who lived.

Brian hadn't spoken to Langley in more than a year.

Langley put the letter back into the envelope and looked out the window again. He was warm and dry inside his office. The radiator let off some steam, and he sat motionless for a moment or two.

He was absolutely unsure about what he was going to do next when his phone rang. He looked at the phone, and all it said was "private number." But he was used to that.

"Hello," said Langley as he put his brother's letter in the top drawer of his desk. There was silence at the other end of the phone. "Hello?"

"Mr. Calhoun?"

"Yes?" he said. "Hello?"

"I'm Lucy Williams," the voice said. Langley expected something more, but there was only silence. When he started to say something, the voice said, "We used to know each other."

Langley knew the name. Ned Williams, a friend of his when they were kids, had a sister named Lucy. She was a few years younger, but he didn't really know her. When you're nine years old the difference of a couple of years is an entire lifetime.

There was another pause. "How can I—Lucy? How can I help you?"

"The reason I'm calling is, well …" and there was a long pause.

Langley waited for her to say something and finally said again, "Hello?"

"I was wondering if you had any time to meet with me."

He paused. "What, ah ..."

"I'm sick," she suddenly said.

This startled Langley. He waited again, but she didn't say anything.

"I'm sorry. I'm, uh, is there ...?" he said.

"I'm sick, and I would like to talk to someone."

"I'm not sure. I don't ... is there a problem?" He put his hand over his face and wondered, very quickly, what he could do to avoid whatever it was that Lucy was about to ask him. His words came out badly and unformed, and he kept his hand over his eyes as if to shield himself from whatever bad news she was going to tell him.

"Can you talk to me?"

"I mean, Lucy, if you're sick, it ..."

"I just would like to talk to you."

Three

6:00 p.m., Fenton, New Hampshire. Lucy Williams sat on the edge of her seat, quite literally, as though she was going to bolt out of Langley's truck any second. She seemed like she was on the verge of tears. She didn't speak. Her hair was matted, her face was thin and pale, and she had on a faint trace of red lipstick that only made her look worse. Her clothes were rumpled and dirty.

"I'm not well," she said simply, holding her coat softly in her lap. They were sitting in his truck in front of her house. The rain had stopped, but it was still cold and raw outside.

"I'm sorry," said Langley. He knew sitting there like that would send the signal that he wasn't ready to commit to anything she might ask of him, but in the past year he had become more cautious, less open, and so he was going to tread warily when it came to whatever Lucy Williams was trying to get across.

"My father ... " she said softly, thoughtfully, putting her head down.

Langley did not like the sound of that. He suddenly realized he didn't know if her illness was biological or mental. He didn't know what to expect.

"Things have not been going well," she said.

He didn't know what to do. He knew the Williams family was deeply troubled and had been plagued—that seemed to be the right word—with illness and trauma. Her brother Ned, the kid Langley had been friends with, had committed suicide a long time ago, and there was always a rumor or two about other things. Both her mother and father had died young. He had sometimes quietly hoped Lucy had escaped the family fate.

"You know. My family has always been afflicted with, well ... " Her voice trailed off into a whisper.

Langley just shook his head. and took in a deep breath. "What is it that I can do for you?" He didn't mean for that to sound cold and abrupt, but it did.

"I don't know," she said. "I just wanted someone to talk to, and every time I saw you in the neighborhood or on TV, you always seemed so kind."

Langley didn't know what to say. His time in the spotlight had been a couple of years ago. Kind. It was not the first word people used to describe a guy who had put his own brother in jail. He certainly didn't think he was as nice any more. He was much less willing to be the kind and patient public servant that he had been for all those years and she expected him still to be.

"You remember my uncle Terry, he was my father's brother, he lived two doors down from here."

"I remember him."

"He died of Lou Gehrig's disease three years ago," she said.

Langley closed his eyes and then opened them.

"Everyone just keeps saying it's my family."

"What are they saying?" said Langley.

"There is something wrong with this neighborhood, and it's because of the Oquossoc. There's something wrong with the river." The Oquossoc was the river that ran through the town of Fenton. This little neighborhood in Fenton she was talking about was called the Shoals, and it edged up right against the banks of the river. They were sitting in front of Lucy's house, and the bend in the river was right across the street.

"I am going to die, and I wanted to tell you that because I wanted someone to know who wouldn't forget it."

"Is your condition that bad?"

Lucy sighed. "Yes."

"What is it you'd like me to do?" said Langley.

"I'm not related to the Marabellas, and both Mr. and Mrs. Marabella have had health problems." Her conversation was jumping around, confused. Langley kept the tone of his voice calm.

"I knew them," he said about the Marabellas. "I knew them." This was a couple who lived in the neighborhood. When they were kids, everyone thought they were slightly creepy.

"The water," she said suddenly. "There are just so many things." It was then she started to cry. "I'm sorry," she said. It was a bad habit some people had, saying they were sorry for crying in public. No one should ever say they're sorry for crying in front of another person. When she put her hands to her face Langley could see the skin was cracked and dry. It looked painful.

"What can I do?"

"There has to be a reason for this, a source for it. I think it's the river. It's polluted. It's dirty."

"It's exactly the opposite," said Langley, and it was true. Decades ago the Oquossoc had been so dirty no one could swim in it. But the tanning companies and the electric light bulb manufacturer that operated along the banks of the river had closed years ago, the buildings had been razed, and the river had slowly cleaned itself out.

There was one small mill building left called The Dryhouse, but it was empty and just a relic, a remembrance of old New England. It was the place where they had dried the leather. You could see it from Lucy's house; it wasn't three hundred yards away. But it had been empty for more than sixty years.

"No, it's dirty," she said.

"Everybody swims in the Oquossoc. I swam in it," said Langley. "People fish out of it."

"What do you really know?" said Lucy. "Something is happening to me."

Langley leaned back. It was impossible to argue with that. If you lived on a planet of seven billion people, and you were the only one who was sick, nothing else would matter. He was sorry that he'd kept his truck running. It must have seemed as though he wanted to get rid of her. Langley shut his engine off. He pushed a button to roll down his window slightly because it was fogging up.

Langley wanted to tell her that it could be just bad luck, but he didn't.

"Who else have you tried to tell?" asked Langley.

"I called the newspaper. I wrote to Maria Tull." Maria Tull was Chairman of the Board of Selectmen in town. "I wrote to …" She simply sighed. "No one cared. I'm just one person who everyone thinks is crazy anyway."

"What did they say?"

"They didn't say anything. No one even got back to me."

"Did you tell them you were sick?"

"That was probably my mistake."

Langley nodded. She was probably right. She was

making an accusation that would have everyone running for cover behind a lawyer.

"I just want you to know," she said. "I want someone to think about this after I'm gone."

"Have you thought about moving?"

"I'm dying, Mr. Calhoun," she said, seemingly shocked he would even mention such a thing. "Moving wouldn't help me now."

Four

Friday, March 8, 7:30 a.m., Durham, NH. Langley was headed over to Delia Reed's apartment with his father. They were in his father's truck. Delia was moving in with him, and they were on their way to start packing her up.

It was a beautiful day. It was exactly the kind of day you should be bouncing along in the passenger seat of a pickup truck in New England. It was the kind of day your lover should be moving in with you.

Langley was still amazed at how much he loved Delia Reed, and he was even more amazed that she loved him. He was feeling happy, and so he decided against telling his father about the letter from Brian.

It was early, and the morning had that spring softness. Everything was soft and fragile, including the light. Tim Calhoun was drinking his coffee, and Langley smelled tobacco.

"What's the deal with the cigarettes?" asked Langley.

"I don't know," said the old man. "It's a hard goddamn thing to break." They drove in silence for a little while. Langley's father had had a serious heart attack a few years ago and shouldn't be smoking.

"How does Vance feel about you smoking?" Vance was the old man's girlfriend.

Tim Calhoun just shot his son a glance as if to say, how do you think she feels about it?

"Dad," said Langley. "Have you ever heard about some crazy shit going on over at the Shoals?"

"What kind of crazy shit?"

"Did you ever hear anything about the Williams family or the Marabellas or anything else going on over there?"

"Those crazy fucks."

"That's what I mean."

"Alcoholic, paranoid, criminal. Ned Williams was a mean son-of-a-bitch, I'll tell you that, and it was no surprise that he killed himself. Probably hated himself more than anybody." Ned Williams was also the name of Lucy Williams' father.

"How polluted was the Oquossoc, really?"

"I'm not following you."

"I saw Lucy Williams the other day."

"Lucy Williams. Christ."

"She's dying."

His father made a face.

"She said that she thought the Oquossoc was making her sick, was making everyone sick over there."

"Of course the Oquossoc was polluted. Christ, there were tanning companies up and down the … that's what Fenton was famous for. Leather. The place was a cesspool, but it isn't any more."

"You ever hear about anybody getting sick from the river before?"

"Sick? From the river?"

"She's got cancer."

"The Williams kids were always so crazy, I'm not surprised she would think the river could make her sick."

Langley shook his head. "She's scared and sick."

"I don't know," his father said somewhat sadly, somewhat wearily. "I don't know."

Five

Same day, 8:15 a.m., Durham, NH. Delia was waiting for them in front of her apartment building. Tim Calhoun kissed her on the forehead and said, "I'm going to pick up Vance." He got back in his truck and drove off. Delia had a cup of coffee in her hand. Delia and Langley looked at each other.

"So," she said.

Langley smiled. "I'm not backing out, if that's what you think."

Delia smiled and kissed him.

"What are we doing out here?" Langley asked.

"I just wanted to say something."

"I know. You get cranky if you don't have your coffee in the morning."

She looked at him and smiled. "That's right," she said with some surprise in her voice, "but that isn't what I was going to say." She and Langley were in each other's arms, and Langley was looking at her beautiful face. "Everything that has ever meant anything to me is up in that apartment," she said.

Langley nodded. "I'm not going to break anything," he said slowly and skeptically.

She smiled. "I'm not worried about you breaking anything." She kissed him again. "It's just that you're going to be packing up things, my things, all of my stuff, and you're going to wonder, where did this come from, and what is the significance of that, and who gave me what."

He looked away from her. "I won't."

"Honey, you're a cop."

"Not anymore."

"Well, then, you're a private investigator, which is more wary and suspicious."

His expression didn't change.

"If we get back to your house with all this stuff, and you see something of mine that I put out on a shelf, and it makes you ... unhappy, just tell me about it, and then we'll deal with it, okay? I just don't want you to start to stomp around not speaking to me only because you're mad about some fucking knick-knack a boyfriend gave me is out on my bureau."

"You had a boyfriend?"

"Ha ha."

"And I don't stomp around."

"No, you don't. You get all quiet and withdrawn."

Langley made a face.

"Okay?"

"We've got some boxes to move," he said.

Delia grabbed him by the arm to stop him. "Okay?" She looked at him. "I'm moving into your house, but I want to feel it's my home."

He nodded again.

In the living room Delia put on a CD, Steely Dan's "Aja," and he could hear her singing along with it. He picked up a plate and wrapped a newspaper around it and put it into the bottom of the box. Jesus, he thought to himself as he looked at the near-empty box and the cabinet before him that was filled with plates, cups, bowls, saucers, glasses. There was a little piece of paper taped inside one of the cabinet doors. The paper was curled and the tape was yellow.

"Have known the evenings, mornings, afternoons, I have measured out my life with coffee spoons." He picked up another plate and stared at it. Transparent, pale green glass with hand-painted flowers.

Julia, Langley's ex-wife, had taken almost none of the china or any of the kitchen stuff with her. Her new husband down in Pennsylvania had a brand new house full of brand new things, and she didn't have to take any of her past life with her. So Langley had settings for four and more that they had bought for all those evenings when Julia wanted to entertain. Langley never seemed to be in the mood to entertain.

He remembered Julia looking at him and saying, "Can't we have some people over just once?"

And Langley, sitting in a chair in their old house, unable or unwilling to answer, and Julia staring at him and then finally turning away with a sigh and tightness in her shoulders, and Langley wanting to get up and tell her, "Yes, please, let's have a party," but for some reason he never could. To this day, he …

"Hey," said Delia.

"Hey," said Langley, breaking out of his reverie.

"Z is coming over." This was Delia's friend Zemira.

Just then there was a knock on the door. Delia and Langley went to answer it, and Langley's father and his girlfriend Vance came into the living room. Vance was carrying a box of coffee from Dunkin' Donuts, and Tim had a box of Munchkins. Everybody hugged, Vance poured everyone a cup of coffee, and Langley ate a donut hole.

"Where do you want us?" said Vance.

"Vance, if you can keep my friend here," Delia looked at Langley, "on track with the dishes in the kitchen, I would be grateful."

Vance grabbed Langley by the hand.

"Your father and I will figure out things in here," said Delia.

"I don't want you to lift anything heavy," Vance said to the old man.

Vance and Langley went into the kitchen. Vance looked into the box and saw just one wrapped plate. "Hmm," she said and looked at Langley, and they both burst out laughing.

"If you could do us a favor," Vance said.

"Sure," said Langley.

"Tape up a few of those packing boxes, get them nice and sturdy, and then we can just keep moving once we start to wrap these dishes up," said Vance.

Keep moving, Langley thought to himself. Keep moving.

Six

Tuesday, March 12, 8:00 a.m., Route 101 toward Manchester, NH. When Langley's phone rang he saw that it was Ed Lustig calling.

"Are you in the office?" Lustig asked.

"Almost," said Langley.

"I'm gonna be a little late."

"What's up?"

"I got pulled over by the cops." There was a pause. "Ah, the little bastard's coming back now."

"What — Ed?"

"This is getting very old," Ed said. Then he hung up.

Langley had worked for Ed Lustig for the past couple of years, but it was only recently that Langley had agreed to work out of Ed's law office, Ed being the only other employee. He had gotten his private investigator's license after his contract wasn't renewed as Chief of Police in Fenton, and during the very first case he worked on Langley had gotten shot.

It had taken some persuading to continue, but Ed Lustig was a persuasive man, and anyway, Langley liked him and wanted to keep busy.

When Ed arrived in the office about a half hour later, he came down the hall to Langley's office and told Langley he needed him. Langley wasn't going to ask him why he got pulled over. He could tell Ed wasn't in the mood to talk.

Langley took his sports jacket off the back of his chair

and put it on as they walked back to Lustig's office. Ed told Langley what was happening as they walked down the hall.

"These two people, a couple, were clients of mine. Their niece has disappeared," Lustig said.

"Living with them?" Langley touched Ed on the arm, and they stopped walking. "Hold on."

"Yes."

"When did she go missing?"

"Coupla nights ago."

"Have they talked to the police?"

"I get the feeling the kid is not so much missing as she is staying with someone they don't like." Lustig was whispering.

They walked into Lustig's office, which had the odor of fresh cigarette smoke. Langley saw the couple, maybe in their early forties but looking older, both sitting in their chairs looking nervous and exhausted.

"Langley Calhoun, this is Fred and Catherine Fahnestock. Langley is a former police officer who now works for me as an investigator."

Langley leaned in and shook their hands. They did not stand up. Their eyes were shifting all over the place. Their palms were cold and sweaty.

Langley sat in the chair against the wall to face them. Lustig took the chair behind his desk. The woman was clutching her purse. The man was scratching the fabric of his pants with his fingernails. The back of the cuffs on his gray slacks were frayed and dirty because he wore pants that were too long for him. The couple looked at each other nervously.

"Just, if you can, just give a quick overview of your situation," said Lustig.

They both started to talk at once. The Fahnestocks looked at each other, and the man then nodded to his wife. He looked down, and she started to speak.

"Our niece Alene has been staying with us for a few weeks, and she, well, she's been having trouble at school."

"Alene, did you say?" said Langley. "I'm sorry, but I just want to get the name right." He took out the pocket-sized spiral-bound notebook that he always carried and wrote in with a small pencil, like the one you'd use to keep score in golf.

"Yes," said Mrs. Fahnestock, and then she spelled it. She took out a school photo of the girl and handed it to Langley. The picture was of one of the most beautiful young women Langley had ever seen. He made no expression as he handed the photo to Ed, who raised his eyebrows.

"We don't have any children of our own, and we've always loved Alene, of course, and we thought we could help. But what ..."

"I'm sorry," said Langley. "Alene is your niece on whose side? What is the relationship?"

"She's my sister Liv's daughter. Liv is in Wisconsin, and she's been a single mom for most of Alene's life. Her husband left not long after Alene was born." Mr. Fahnestock nodded his head in agreement. "We'd call Liv every once in a while, talk to her, talk to Alene, but we never got the sense that anything was wrong. Not really wrong."

"Just tell us what happened."

"Alene started to call us maybe two months ago to tell us how she couldn't stand it out there anymore."

"What was the problem specifically?"

"Oh, just family things, mother and daughter things. Liv didn't think it was anything too out of the ordinary, only that they were at each other nonstop."

"And Alene said she wanted to come live with you," Langley said.

"We said you need to talk to your mother," said Mr. Fahnestock. Here the couple looked at each other.

"So it was Alene's idea to come live with you?"

"Liv finally called us a few weeks ago and said things had really gotten bad, and Alene was begging her to let her come out here," said Mrs. Fahnestock.

"We had always had a great relationship with Alene every time we saw her," said the husband. "Even though Liv had told us what was going on, it was hard to really ..."

"You didn't think the problem was as bad as your sister said it was."

"Right," said the husband, "plus anything seemed better than home at that point. For Alene, I mean. So we thought she was exaggerating."

"You visit for a week in their own home, and everyone is on their best behavior. You forget what it might be like ... " said Catherine Fahnestock.

"So when she came to stay with you?"

"Well, we hadn't seen her in two years, and I don't know how much experience you have with teenage girls, Mr. Calhoun, but the last time we saw Alene was when she was thirteen. She was always very pretty, but when she arrived at our house she was just about to turn sixteen."

Langley thought about how different both his girls seemed every time he saw a new picture of them. They had been growing up without him, and he knew how kids could change even if the last time you saw them was only a little while ago. Langley knew how extreme some changes can seem when contact is so infrequent. Each time he talked to one of his daughters, her voice and her words seemed different from the time before.

And so Langley said, "No, I don't have much experience with teenagers." Ed Lustig looked up when he heard that.

"The difference between when she was thirteen to what she looks like now, well, you can see by the picture. So when we saw her at the airport, we both knew we were in for more then we bargained for," said Catherine. "It seemed like we got along fine. We went out to eat together when we could, if only because we thought it would be boring for her to eat at home with just us old folks." The couple looked at each other and smiled. "We don't have any children."

"Do you know who she met or what she did when she was not in school?"

"She didn't go anywhere. She was really good, stayed on the computer. She has a million friends on the computer," said Catherine.

Langley had no doubt about that. He was also trying to figure out if these answers seemed rehearsed. Something told him the answers sounded planned out. There was something disingenuous about it all, but he couldn't put his finger on it. Maybe they were just nervous. By this time in the conversation the husband had dug his fingers into this thigh.

"We did suggest she get a part-time job," Fred Fahnestock said suddenly. "We asked her to pay fifty dollars a month toward food and cable. You know, nothing too much but enough so she'd have to put in a few hours somewhere after school, you know, to keep things on an even keel."

On an even keel. That was an expression Langley's brother Brian used all the time. He hated that expression.

"Did she get a job?"

"She picked up a couple of shifts at LaRivier's."

"Which one?"

"The one in Hampton on River Rock Road." They looked at each other as if to reassure themselves they were giving the correct information. LaRivier's was a pharmacy chain.

Langley was writing it down in his little notebook. "But other than that, you weren't being overly strict?"

"Other than the job, we didn't really say anything," said Fred Fahnestock, "There was no reason to say anything, Mr. Calhoun. We thought everything was fine until she left."

"She just disappeared," said Langley.

They nodded their heads. "She didn't come home from school the next day."

"That was when?"

"Three nights ago."

"Have you gone to the police?"

"Not yet." Fred Fahnestock sighed. "She texted my wife and said she was all right, that she was with someone."

Langley looked up, surprised. "So you've been in touch?"

"Yes."

"Just that once?"

"Several times."

Langley looked at Lustig. He shook his head. "You could have said that up front." He took the picture back from Ed. "What is it you'd like us to do?" Langley asked flatly.

"Find her."

"This is a family issue, Mrs. Fahnestock. She's not missing. She's gone to live with someone."

"Her father."

"Her father?"

"We think she's with the father."

Langley breathed in deeply. He was frustrated. "You could have said that up front, too. Where's the father?"

"She's a minor, Mr. Calhoun, and he severed all his parental rights years ago."

Family situations. He hated them. "Where is he?"

"We don't know. That's the thing. If she's with him, she shouldn't be, and no one knows where he lives."

"What kind of man is the father?"

"He's a musician."

That's a hell of an answer, Langley wanted to say. "What's the father's name?"

"Joseph Chechik. Joe."

"Spell that."

They did.

"Do you know him at all?"

"Not really."

"Did she ever talk about her father?"

"All the time," said Fred Fahnestock. "She listened to his music. One of the first things she said when she got out here was that she was glad to be closer to her dad, but we just took that as, you know, directed at Liv. Alene was going to, you know, play them against each other."

This all seemed very strange to Langley, but he did not change his expression, nor did he look at Lustig.

"He's a musician? What kind?"

"He's an aging rock star wannabe, apparently," said Fred Fahnestock. He said it with too much rancor, though, too much for a man he said he didn't know. There was something else here, thought Langley.

"You don't like him?" Langley said casually, not looking up from his notebook.

"Not particularly. I mean, it's okay to have a dream, but maybe at some point you should give it up."

"Alene idolizes him," said Catherine Fahnestock quickly.

Langley took their contact information and the cell phone number for Alene. He asked for the phone number of Catherine's sister out in Wisconsin.

They left, mumbling and shuffling out the door in what Langley thought was a too-obvious display of humility and gratitude, and he watched as they walked out and got into their blue Nissan Altima. He looked at the photo again.

"How does a girl who looks like that disappear?"

"She doesn't," said Lustig. "She hasn't. We just don't know where she is."

"They seemed rehearsed," Langley said of the Fahnestocks.

"Everybody in this office seems rehearsed," said Lustig. "You should see them when their checks bounce."

Seven

Thursday, March 21, 6:00 p.m., Langley and Delia's house, Fenton, NH. There were boxes in every room of the house. There were lamps and piles of clothes and tables and furniture everywhere.

"So much stuff," Delia said, and Langley was thinking the exact same thing. He had thought those very words almost at the same time she said them.

Langley was looking at the empty walls. He had exactly one picture hung up in his living room, a photo of him standing with Julia and the kids, Nancy and Patty, in front of a Christmas tree. It wasn't a picture he liked any more than the others he had stored in the basement and the attic. When he had hung it, he'd suddenly realized that having pictures of his estranged family made him feel lonely and distant. So that was the only one he had hung.

Delia had beautiful pictures, though. Framed pictures of plants and birds and landscapes. She had a beautiful watercolor of a Japanese iris that was elegant and simple. There was a pencil sketch of a fierce owl swooping down on a branch. There was a tiny old oil painting of a landscape of a river that was no bigger than a postcard. It could have been a look at the bend in the Oquossoc as it looked two hundred years ago.

Langley opened one of the boxes carefully. The contents were obscured by tufts of old, bunched up newspapers that concealed Delia's treasures.

"This couple came into the office today," he said.

Delia was picking through some stuff, and when he didn't say anything more, she asked, "What did they want?"

"Their niece has disappeared."

"They want you to find her?"

"Complicated family situation."

"That's what you do, isn't it?"

"Take a look at this." Langley handed Delia the photo of Alene.

She looked at it. "Wow." She handed it back to Langley.

"She's apparently with her father somewhere."

Delia stopped doing what she was doing and looked at him. "What about Lucy?"

Lucy Williams. Langley shook his head. "I should call her."

"You promised her you would," Delia said.

He unpacked a few more things, feeling awkward, and Delia suddenly said, "Do you feel awkward at all?"

Langley shook his head again, not because he was answering her question, but because he was startled that she was seemingly reading his mind. He did feel awkward, and he did feel like there was a lot of stuff.

His inclination was to say no, everything was fine, that he was excited she was moving in. But he looked into her green eyes and said, "I think one of the things I want to do is go through my own stuff. See what we can get rid of, see what stuff maybe Julia and the girls might want."

Delia nodded.

"There may be some things they didn't want when they left, but they may want now," he said.

"Do you want me to wait before I really start to unpack?"

"No, no," Langley said while also letting out a long, exhaustive breath. "I need you to get in here."

Delia looked around the room.

"Let me ask you a question," Langley said. "Is there anything around here that you can't stand?" He stood looking at Delia, and when she saw how innocent and serious he was, she burst out laughing.

"Oh, honey, the place has so much style."

Langley laughed, too, but he knew things had really changed when he got up in the middle of the night and went into the bathroom. He wasn't sleeping well. He turned on the light and stood still for a moment. The bathroom hadn't changed much. There was a new towel, and Delia's things were on the sink, but those things had been there for some time. But something seemed very, very different.

He stood for a moment in the middle of the small, white room and realized the place smelled mildly and sweetly of coconut. He had told Delia that was one of his favorite aromas months and months ago.

Eight

Thursday, March 28, noon, Ed Lustig's office.   When
Langley Googled "Joe Chechik musician," he was thankful
that the guy had an unusual name.

A long list of responses for Joe Chechik came up,
primarily club listings where Chechik had played over the
past several years. He was either the headliner or part of a
pickup band in small clubs. He played all over the country,
including some recent dates in New England. He had a
website that sold his CDs, mostly with romantic street poet-
type titles like *Man of the Road* and *At The Lonely Hotel.*
Joe Chechik clearly sought himself as a descendent of Bob
Dylan and other roving troubadours.

Langley was sitting at his desk, and his computer
monitor was glowing. There was an email address on the
site that Langley clicked on. It was active, and Langley
wrote it down. Chechik's cell phone number had an area
code of 920, which was in Green Bay, Wisconsin, but that
didn't mean Joe Chechik was actually in Green Bay,
Wisconsin.

There were some links to Chechik's songs, and Langley
clicked on one to listen to one called "This is you." It was
an okay tune, Langley thought, and when he listened to
another he could hear that Joe Chechik had a certain
amount of talent but nothing that was going to set him apart
from a million other lonely singer-songwriters out there.

It was like those watercolors you see at the local art club. They're okay, and you only really buy one if you know the artist.

On Chechik's site there were links to a couple of articles in newspapers out of Wisconsin detailing his pursuit of reality TV stardom. He had tried out for several singing programs, but there weren't any articles announcing that Chechik had won a spot on any of them.

The photos of Chechik, and there were many, showed a guy trying too hard to be a rock star. He was not handsome. He didn't have quite the right look for a singing star. If you stripped away the jewelry and the black clothes and the sneer and the stubble, you'd have a choir boy. You can get away with that maybe if you have talent, but if you don't, you had better be better looking than Joe Chechik.

Langley saw something else. As Joe Chechik aged in the photos, something slightly sinister started to creep into the man's face. The younger expressions, the insouciance, became a little more forced, a little less sincere, and Langley could see, as he clicked on twenty years worth of photos, the fun drain out of Joe Chechik's smile. His posture started to slump. Lack of success had taken its toll on Joe Chechik, and it was getting harder and harder to hide it.

Langley's phone rang, and the caller was listed as a "private number." He pushed the talk button and said hello. There was silence on the other end of the line. Langley was not going to say hello again. He waited a few more moments and hung up. It might have been Lucy Williams. He wished he had her number so he could call her back, but she wouldn't give it to him.

It looked as though Chechik's career had slowed to a

stop a few months ago. There were no recent gigs mentioned, and the time between each of the more recent gigs got longer and longer. A week, two weeks, now a month, even longer. This is how a middling career winds down. No new material. No hit records, no reality TV, and a slew of kids with new bands with new sounds kicking you to the curb. You can't have the swagger of the next up and coming thing or an undiscovered genius when you're closing in on forty-five years old.

Langley looked up different combinations on the web, "Joe Chechik teacher," "Joe Chechik music teacher," "Joe Chechik arrest," and nothing new came up. It's one thing for a career to wind down, thought Langley, but where had the guy gone to?

Langley then Googled the name "Alene Chechik," and to his surprise there was another "Alene Chechik," a middle-aged woman in Arizona who had a Facebook page. What were the odds of that?

The Alene Chechik he was looking for had her own Facebook page, but Langley could not see her information because he was not her "friend." He decided to send her a friend request. She would either accept it without thinking, or she would find out who he was and know that someone was looking for her.

Nine

Same day, 3:00 p.m., Ed Lustig's office. Langley called Liv Olson, Catherine Fahnestock's sister, and when she picked up the phone Langley heard a tired, miserable voice. He introduced himself and said he had been hired by the Fahnestocks to help find her daughter.

Langley asked if she had heard from her daughter or Joe Chechik.

"The last time he called me up he was drunk or high, and he was complaining about how miserable he was. He's yelling. He calls me after a gig, you know. He can't pick up the girls the way he used to, so after one of his awful little gigs, you know, from Scranton or someplace, he calls me up, and he talks about how miserable his life is."

"What do you tell him?"

"I don't say nothing. He doesn't let me say nothing. He starts out very sweet and tender, and then when I don't agree to have phone sex with him, he turns abusive and stupid, so I hang up."

"Why does he call?"

"Because I'm the only girl left that will speak to him at two in the morning," she said, "but I know Alene is with him now because he hasn't called in days."

"You have no idea where he lives, where they could be?" Langley asked.

"I bet he's right there in New Hampshire. That's why Alene went out there. That's why we hired you. She didn't

go out there to live with my sister and that husband of
hers."

"If you hear from him again, let me know."

"Don't you think I know that?"

Langley ended the call and walked into Lustig's office.
Lustig was opening a new pack of cigarettes.

"The mother, Catherine Fahnestock's sister, definitely
thinks Alene and the father are together. Here in New
Hampshire."

"Find the father, find the girl."

"This is a funny one," said Langley.

"I think the kid just wanted to stick it to the mother, and
the old man is taking advantage of that. He'll run to her
rescue, thinking it'll make up for not having been a father to
the kid for all these years."

"Maybe," said Langley. He had his own making up to
do with his children. "But why disappear? What's the
reason for dropping off the grid when you know it could
only lead to trouble?"

Ten

Same day, 4:00 p.m., Fenton, NH. Langley walked up the old flagstone path to the door of Lucy Williams' house. The lawn was weedy and brown. The paint on the windowsills had long since cracked and curled, and some of the wood was rotting away. This was not the kind of house you should live in if you can't afford it, thought Langley, because when you can't afford it things go to shit. Lucy clearly could not afford living in this house.

He pushed the doorbell and waited. He pushed it again but realized he didn't hear any bell or buzz. He pressed the little white button, but it was silent. He stepped away from the door and looked up. The shade in the middle window on the second floor was torn. He looked down and sighed and went back up to the door and knocked on it.

"Lucy? Lucy Williams?" He waited with his knuckles poised a few inches away from the door. He knocked again and called out, "It's Langley Calhoun."

He waited with his head tilted down, as though that position would help him hear better. He didn't hear a thing. He stepped back and shouted "Lucy?" but again there was nothing.

When Langley turned to get into his car, he saw for the first time the construction crew working near the old, red covered bridge that spanned the Oquossoc. It looked as if the crew was working toward actually removing the bridge, but Langley knew that couldn't be right. The bridge was only a few hundred yards from Lucy's house.

He didn't have a chance to think any more about it because he heard the sound of Lucy Williams' voice.

Eleven

Same day, 4:35 p.m. "Hi," said Langley. Lucy was at the front door of her house, but she hadn't opened it. She hadn't replaced the screen door when the winter came.

"Hi," she said sweetly. "I was just thinking about you."

Langley walked up to the door. "I just came by to see how you're doing."

"I'm fine," she said, but she was wary.

"Do you have time to talk?"

She thought for a second and then said, "The house is a little, um, it's kind of ..."

"We can go somewhere, if you'd like." Langley wondered if she was up to it. It was cold, and she looked so fragile.

But then she said, "Let me get my coat." She left the inside door open only a crack, and Langley tried to get a look inside through the screen, but the light wasn't in his favor, and everything was in shadow.

Lucy returned wearing an overcoat, and she was wrapping a handmade knitted scarf around her neck. She came out the door and closed it behind her. She looked at Langley furtively, shyly.

"Where would you like to go?"

"I don't care," she said softly, "anywhere that you'd like."

"We can go over to the Old Brown Tree," he suggested, naming a local tavern. It was only eleven o'clock in the morning, but she didn't protest.

The Old Brown Tree Pub was unofficially known as the smallest bar in the world. It had opened in 1918 and had only eight stools and four tables. Its maximum legal capacity was twenty-four people. It was just a narrow little slit in the side of an old stone building, and all you could get was wine and the brewed ale known as Old Brown Tree. Langley and the other cops used to drink there after hours when he was on the force.

The Old Brown Tree only took cash. It was one of the few places where, if the bar and tables were full, you could see cash lying in front of the patrons. There would be cash, perspiration rings from the glasses and bottles, assorted pocket change and packs of cigarettes on the bar. People had to go outside to smoke, but the owner-bartender, Sean, let people smoke inside if it was late, and there was no one else in the pub who minded. Ale was five dollars a pint, served in a smooth, cold glass.

When they walked in Sean looked up from his newspaper. "Good morning, good morning," he said. He had just opened. "Chief," Sean said, nodding. "Hello," he said to Lucy Williams. When he said hello to Lucy she smiled so sweetly and happily, it almost broke Langley's heart.

"Hey, Sean," said Langley. Lucy nodded silently.

"What are you two going to have?"

"I'd like a glass of cabernet," Lucy said without looking up.

"And I'll have a pint," said Langley. "Pickled egg, if you've got it."

Lucy smiled a wan little smile and kept looking down at her lap. Their drinks were put in front of them. The pickled egg, shiny and wet and slightly blue, rolled about on a teacup saucer. Sean went back to reading the paper. They were the only three people in the bar.

"What do you do?" Langley asked Lucy. She looked up at him and smiled. "What's your job, I mean?"

"I haven't been able to work in a year," she said. "I can't."

"How do you support yourself?"

"I'm on disability, SSI," she said. "I sometimes get so scared about what will happen. What will happen to me," she said.

They stared at their drinks. Langley could tell that Sean had stopped reading the paper and was listening to them, even though he was still staring at the page.

"Is there anybody in your family around?"

"Not anymore."

The Williams family had an unusual amount of bad luck.

"I was looking at the Oquossoc the other day, and you know what I thought?"

"No," said Langley.

"I was thinking how the water washes out to the ocean, and how it evaporates and drifts up into the clouds, and how it falls back to the earth again, over and over and over, and how it makes everything grow, and how it made life begin," Lucy said, her voice very far away but sweet. "I was thinking about how we are made out of nothing but rain. All we are," she said, "is rain."

Langley thought these were the last plaintive thoughts of a dying woman. It must be what she thinks about looking out the window, feeling her body dry up.

They sat and talked for a little while. They remembered

their old middle school, which was now a community building, and who they had known together and if they kept up with anyone. The conversation was slow but not forced, and Langley was unnerved at how thin and gaunt Lucy was, but he felt that she was glad to talk to somebody. Maybe that was the job she wanted him to do.

"I'm glad we met again," she said finally.

"I am, too," Langley said.

"Pretty soon I'm going to stop my treatments, and then ..." But she didn't finish her sentence. She finally said. "I'll call you."

"I can call you, too," Langley said.

"I have a private number. You'll know it's me if I call. I won't bother you."

"You're not bothering me," Langley said, and he meant it. "I'll be happy to meet you again. You asked me to do something. I'll see what I can do about what's in the river."

"It's okay," she said, and the fingers of her left hand reached out and brushed Langley's arm in a lovely little moment of flirtation and connection.

They asked Sean for the check, and he put a piece of paper in front of them.

"Let me help with that," said Lucy. She took out four crumpled one dollar bills. They stood, nodded at Sean and left the Old Brown Tree.

Lucy hadn't touched her wine.

Twelve

Wednesday, April 3, 4:00 p.m., Portsmouth, NH. Langley drove through Fenton and went over the Piscataqua River on the Route 95 bridge into Portsmouth. When he rode over the bridge he looked down at the big river, known to have one of the most powerful currents in the world, but which was now quiet. A clear, blue sky was above him.

He drove down Congress Street, and as he was looking for a parking spot he saw a woman leaning into her parked car. All Langley really saw was a skirt and two strong legs, and she was bent over at a ninety-degree angle. Langley kept staring at her because he had this habit of always wanting to see a person's face, but she hadn't found what she was looking for by the time Langley passed. All he would ever see was the short gray skirt, too short for this time of year, and a pair of legs he wouldn't soon forget.

He parked over on State Street in the center of town and walked into Blue Bear Records, which was an old style music store. There were stickers for CDs pasted all over the windows, as well as handmade posters for upcoming gigs and CD release parties and concerts and local theater. The carpet on the floor of the shop was a mess, and there were posters for obscure bands — obscure to Langley — all over the walls.

Langley looked in the bins, in which CDs were arranged alphabetically. Joe Chechik was a folk musician, a balladeer, a singer-songwriter, so Langley looked in those sections, but he couldn't find anything. Not even a used CD.

He looked in the local music section, but there was nothing there either. He asked the clerk, who looked up the name in his computer and shook his head. Chechik was listed in their database, but they didn't have anything in stock.

Langley knew there was no reason to go over to Walmart or Barnes & Noble, because Chechik was too far down the pecking order to get any space there.

He went back home. Even though it was quiet in the house, it seemed unsettled. There were boxes everywhere. Langley hadn't been much help unpacking. Delia was at work.

Langley opened his laptop and clicked on Joe Chechik's website again. A link on the website said Chechik's albums were released through Rock City Records. The phone number had a 610 area code, which was also out in Wisconsin. Fucking Wisconsin, thought Langley. He looked at his watch to see what the time difference would be.

He dialed the phone and heard an affable voice. "Rock City Records."

"Yeah, I'm wondering if you could help me. I'm looking for the most recent record by Joe Chechik — Chechik? I hope I'm getting the name right."

"Joey, Joey ... yeah, you have it right. Rock and roll Chechik. I'm assuming you're looking for the most recent, right?"

"Uh huh, yeah, my ... "

"You're not looking for any of the solo stuff?"

"Well, yeah, solo ... "

"You want the new band stuff? His new band?"

"I only want the most recent album."

"Yeah, album, the most recent album, sure," said the kid, laughing. "The most recent *al-bum,*" and even Langley had to laugh about how he was getting his balls busted, "the most recent album is Checkmate. Checkmate."

"Excuse me?"

"Dude has a band called Checkmate. That's what he's recording under, Checkmate. Or at least he was. This *al-bum* is three years old."

"Right, right. Checkmate. That's it."

"Different name, same game," the kid said. "What are you, like, his brother or something?"

"No, why?"

"Because nobody ever buys this shit, man," the kid said cheerfully.

"How can I get the Checkmate CD?"

"You can order it from me. You can order it from me, man."

"Don't they have a website?"

"You want to order straight from them, go right ahead."

"No, I was just curious."

"Hold on, hold on, hold on." There was a short pause. "Checkmate1234.com." The kid laughed. "They obviously couldn't register checkmate.com. Got to it too late. Old fuckin' guy."

"Okay, thank you," said Langley. He gave the kid his credit card information and ordered the CD.

"Rock on," said the kid, who then hung up.

Langley typed in "checkmate1234.com." Up popped a one-page website, and there was an aging Joe Chechik, aka Joey Cee. There he was. Joe Chechik had been eased out.

He was now Joey Cee, his hair the color of onyx, his muscles newly rippled but covered with chicken skin that is the hardest thing to hide

The website was amateurish, untended to and corny. A couple of the links were supposedly under construction. There were no reviews of the albums, and the "upcoming gigs" page was empty, but Langley didn't care about that. There was nothing on it to tell Langley where Joe Chechik — Joey Cee — might be or where his daughter might be either.

Thirteen

Thursday, April 4, 11:00 a.m., Hampton, NH. It's a hard thing to learn to live life a different way, and that's what Langley Calhoun was trying to do. He was trying to look at his town beyond the margins of a police report. He used to come into contact with most people after they had been accused of something, and so he looked at most people as though they were already guilty.

He was trying to think differently. His inclination was to think the Fahnestocks were doing something wrong, and he was fighting that. He wanted to give them a chance. He even wanted to be wrong about them, but that nagging feeling in the middle of his gut told him he wasn't.

He also wondered if he was off his game. He just couldn't tell if Catherine and Fred Fahnestock were telling the truth. He was wondering what they were up to. He could not figure out what benefit it would be to them to make up a story about their niece going missing, if indeed that was what they were doing. He couldn't understand why Alene and an unknown musician would go into hiding but only in a half-assed way.

He wanted to talk to Fahnestocks, at their house.

They lived in Hampton, on Pancake Pan Road, in a modest ranch-style home that was painted, as Langley thought, borrowing a phrase from Tom Waits, "monkey shit brown." The paint was faded and streaked, and the lawn had patches of dead grass all over it. The house had an air of dissipation.

It was the home of another American family that never quite made it.

Langley knocked on the door. The lights were on inside, and Catherine Fahnestock came to the door. She did not look surprised to see Langley. She let him in and explained that her husband was not home.

The walls in the house were bare. He realized why. In a home like this the walls in the living room and going up the stairs usually would have been filled with pictures of children, those fading color photographs of the kids as they progressed from grammar school through high school, a virtual catalogue of their hairstyles and styles of dress. But there were no children in this house, and so there were no photographs.

"Please sit down," said Mrs. Fahnestock. "Do you have any news?"

"I talked to your sister," said Langley, shaking his head. There was a guitar in the corner of the room.

Mrs. Fahnestock sat on the couch, avoiding Langley's eyes and with her hands folded on her lap.

"Have you talked to her?" Langley asked.

"Not today, no," she said.

"She thinks Alene is with the father."

"How or why does she know that?" She fidgeted.

"She hasn't heard from Chechik in days, so she thinks he now has someone to keep him company, which would be Alene. He usually calls late and drunk. Have you heard from Alene?"

"She texted me, yes."

"Well, that's good. What did she say?" Again, they were supposedly hiding but staying in touch.

"She said she's fine."

"Did you ask her where she was? Did you ask her to come home?"

"No."

That was frustrating. "Why not?"

"I don't know. That's your business."

"Did you know Joe Chechik changed his name?" Langley asked this question casually, but Mrs. Fahnestock seemed so paralyzed by the question, she didn't even answer.

"Look, Mrs. Fahnestock, I want to help you," said Langley.

She nodded in silence.

"Mrs. Fahnestock?"

She looked at Langley with her eyes wide open, as though she was afraid to say anything.

Fourteen

Thursday, April 11, Police Headquarters, Hampton, NH.
"Curt," Langley said as he sat down in the office of Det.
Curt Bugbee of the Hampton Police Department.

"Chief."

They had run into each other here and there over the
years and liked each other. Langley took out two photos,
one of Joe Chechik and one of Alene, and handed them
over to the detective. Bugbee looked at the pictures and
then at Langley. He didn't react one way or the other.

"A couple by the name of Fahnestock walks into the
office of the attorney I work for a few weeks back and tells
a long tale that the niece they're looking after, who is
originally from Wisconsin, has disappeared, and they don't
know what to do," said Langley.

"So they come to you?"

"The girl is Alene Olson, and the father is named Joe
Chechik. The couple that came in seemed more tense than
nervous, and they outlined what caused the kid to come live
with them. They don't know for certain, but everyone
thinks she's with the old man," said Langley, "this failed
musician."

"Chechik?" said Bugbee.

Langley spelled it. "Joseph. Goes by the name of Joey
Cee now. Has put some little independent records out. No
fame, no fortune."

"Jesus," said Bugbee. He was looking up Chechik. "Anything unusual?"

"Nobody in the family seems too worried, you know? They're weird but not worried. Something's wrong."

"So the father and daughter are maybe together?"

"He gave up his parental rights a long time ago. She's underage. That's the deal. But I bet you they're together."

"I don't have anything," said Bugbee, looking away from the computer. "He's not in the system."

"Some rebel," said Langley.

"What do you want to do?"

"Go to the media. You guys put the word out that the cops are now looking for Chechik and his daughter, that it's now serious. I don't know what they're up to, but they won't want any trouble. This family is stringing me along, so I'm cutting them loose."

"Okay. We can do that."

"Good luck," said Langley as he stood, extending his hand.

"We'll see what happens," said Det. Bugbee, shaking it.

As Langley turned to go, he stopped and looked at Bugbee. "Hey, Curt. I have a question."

Bugbee spread his hands apart to welcome the question.

"You know the Oquossoc River that shoots through Fenton and Dover over my way?"

"I know it, sure. Not well, but I know it. Of course."

"Has anybody ever said anything to you about it being polluted?"

"Come again?"

"Have you ever heard, even casually, anything about the Oquossoc being polluted? Anything? Anything weird about it?"

Bugbee thought for a second. "I'm not sure what you mean exactly, but there's never been any kind of investigation or anything like that. I don't think so. Not that I can think of. What's going on?"

Langley shook his head. "Woman came to me a little while ago. Sick. She said the water from the Oquossoc was making her ill. She's dying."

"I'm sorry to hear that, but I haven't heard anything."

"Okay. Thanks."

"Sounds like someone's thinking about a lawsuit," said Bugbee, but Langley knew it was too late for that.

Fifteen

Friday, April 12, 6:00 p.m., Langley and Delia's house.
The next day on the six o'clock news there was a report on
Channel 9 about a missing girl, Alene Olson, 16, who
might possibly be with her father, musician Joe Chechik,
about 45, somewhere in New Hampshire.

The reporter interviewed Catherine Fahnestock, all
nerves and tics, who described Alene as an "aspiring
singer," which was news to Langley. The brief interview
took place in their driveway as they were getting into their
car.

They flashed pictures of both Alene and Joe Chechik,
and Langley knew the photo of Alene would spark a
thousand different imaginations. The good thing is that
there was certainly going to be a reaction.

There was a brief clip of Det. Bugbee, asking the public
to call the police department if they knew anything. He
ominously mentioned the word "kidnapping." Then a
number was flashed on the screen.

Not a minute after the segment ended, Langley's phone
started to ring. The first call he took was from Ed Lustig.

"You finished with the case?" Lustig asked.

"Nope, just trying an angle," said Langley.

"Have you heard from the Fahnestocks?"

"I hope to. I hope the phone rings any second."

The Fahnestocks did not call, and after the segment ran again at eleven o'clock, Langley told Delia he was taking a ride to Hampton to see what was up.

He drove out of Fenton, past the cornfields that fairly glowed in the moonlight, and he went by the Oquossoc River. Just a block away was Lucy Williams' house, which had just one lighted window on the second floor.

Langley drove down Route 33 into Hampton. Driving through the New England countryside relaxed Langley. He was at home here on these gently rolling roads.

Sixteen

Same day, 8:30 p.m., Hampton, NH. There were no cars in the driveway of the Fahnestocks', and the doors to the two-car garage were closed. Langley wanted to see if there was any action over here after the news report. He got out of his truck, put his hand on the handle of his firearm and walked up the path leading to the front door of the Fahnestocks' house.

He opened the screen door, leaned his head in to listen for a moment and then knocked. He knew no one was home. You can feel when a house is empty, and you can feel when someone is inside and trying to hide. You can just feel it either way.

Langley knocked again. He tried the doorknob, but it didn't twist. He backed away from the door and looked up at the house. It was dark and still.

"Hey," said a voice behind him, and Langley wheeled around and almost drew his gun. The man standing behind him put his hands up in a defensive position.

"I'm a neighbor!" The man was almost crouching.

"Get on the ground. Lie down on your stomach and stretch your arms out in front of you," said Langley. The man did just as he was told.

"I was just … "

"Shut up," said Langley. He went over to the man. "Do you have any knives or sharp objects in your pockets? Any needles?"

"No. I'm just the neighbor."

Langley frisked the man and then stepped back. "What's your name?"

"Cameron Paul. I live right across the street, right there." The man was trying to point with his shoulders and his chin. He was shaking.

"Okay," said Langley, patting the man on the back. "Relax." He put his gun away.

The man scrambled to his feet but backed a foot or two extra away from Langley. He was breathing hard. "We had seen the report on the news. My wife and I were looking out the window when we saw you pull up."

"Which one is your house?"

"That one." The man pointed with his finger. "Number 233, the white one." He paused. He was breathing hard.

"Go on."

"We were kind of curious, you know. We didn't know what the hell was going on over here."

"What do you mean, going on over here?"

"I was out front here the day Alene left, and then I see that the Fahnestocks say she's missing."

"What do you mean, the day Alene left?"

"Fred and Cathy were here when she left. They were all here."

"How do you know that?"

"The guy on the news, the guy identified as her father? He was the one that came to pick her up."

"And the Fahnestocks were here when Alene left with her father?"

"They helped pack her up."

"God damn it," said Langley. "I knew it."

Seventeen

Same day, 9:45 p.m., on the road to Fenton, NH. Langley called Det. Bugbee and told him what the neighbor had said.

"It's good they lied to you and not to me," said the detective. "We've got calls coming in now. One was from a guy named Daly who owns a recording studio in Portsmouth saying that if we catch Chechik to tell him he's still owed three thousand bucks."

Langley laughed and hung up.

The story was picked up by the local papers and then by the Associated Press, and pretty soon the news was everywhere. National TV shows like *Today* and *Good Morning America* and CNN and FOX and the other networks were picking it up. *Entertainment Tonight* called Joe Chechik a musician and Alene simply a singer.

The story gained momentum. It took on a kind of weird energy. Classmates of Alene's from Wisconsin were interviewed. When the reporters found out about Langley's involvement, they followed him around, but he had nothing to say.

Old band mates of Joe Chechik were shoving their faces in front of every microphone they could find. They treated it as a lark, an opportunity to get their names out there.

An old home video of young Alene performing a Miley Cyrus song popped up on the entertainment shows. Video of Joe Chechik performing was aired.

Every bit player was getting face time, and all of it was because of Alene's face.

These long-playing family dramas, played out on national TV, had become a new kind of network miniseries. They had huge casts of revolving characters: the victim, the family, the suspect, the cops, the lawyers, the towns in which they lived. The networks were adept at inflating a private tragedy into a sprawling public epic that no one actually had to write or pay the actors to appear in.

Including Alene's mother. She was seemingly on every TV show, every tabloid magazine show, every radio program, Howard Stern. She was an absolute dream of an American stereotype: a cigarette-smoking, bitter, underemployed, half-beaten, forgotten, abandoned human being who nonetheless took to her celebrity as though she had been planning for it her entire life—and indeed, perhaps she had.

"I was going to be an actress," she said on TMZ. "I had my dreams," she said bitterly, her face gaunt and toothless. Past the wrinkles and the bitterness, Langley could see a woman who may have been very pretty once.

"Well, she has her wish now," said Delia when they were watching TV one night. "Look at her, a born star."

Eighteen

Monday, May 6, 9:00 p.m., Langley and Delia's house.
"You need to come to the PD," Det. Bugbee told Langley over the phone.

"What's happening?"

"The circus has come to town," said Bugbee.

The Hampton Police Department on Bunker Hill Road was, by the looks of it when Langley arrived, the center of the universe. There were reporters everywhere. There were hordes of young people with their own video cameras waiting around. They were all trying to crowd into the police station, because it was raining. It was actually a soaking, loud, unrelenting rain, and everybody's clothes and equipment were dripping wet. The floors were wet; everything was damp.

Langley pushed his way through the crowd and tried to find Det. Bugbee. When he found him, Bugbee said, "Alene and Chechik are turning themselves in at ten."

"How did the media find out?"

"We didn't call them," said Bugbee, annoyed.

Langley shook his head. He pressed his fingers over his eyes and wiped the rain away. He went into the bathroom and pulled a few paper towels from the machine and wiped his hair to stop the water from dripping into his eyes.

At just about ten o'clock three people came walking into the station. There was Alene, looking stunning and not at all harried or frightened. She had on a miniskirt, simple white blouse and a denim jacket. Some guy was holding an umbrella over her head, like a functionary for the pope. Her outfit was not meant to keep a body warm against the cold. This was an outfit meant to show the world what she had to offer.

Joe Chechik was next, dressed all in black, and he was waving to the crowd like he was a prizefighter entering the ring for the championship bout, even though he must have known he was not. But Langley laughed. Maybe he didn't really know he was the opening act.

The third person, holding the umbrella, was someone Langley didn't know but instantly recognized as an attorney he had seen on TV.

The media reps were filming and snapping away. Questions were being thrown out, such as where had the girl been? Had she been kept against her will? How is everyone related?

When the trio was inside and standing in front of the crowd, the umbrella closed, with Alene composing herself and Joey Cee mopping himself off because he had not been protected from the rain by an umbrella, the attorney spread out his hands and tried to quiet the crowd.

But Langley was focusing on something he heard behind him. Someone said the whole thing was an act.

Of course this thing was staged, he realized suddenly, and how smart of them to go to a private detective who would set the whole thing up.

Langley could see the lawyer conferring with Bugbee and Hal Merlo, the Hampton Chief of Police. Langley could easily see that the cops were unhappy. They were furious about having their police station turned into a TV studio. The three men nodded, and then Langley could see

Merlo say to the attorney, "Make it fucking quick."

The attorney stood in front of the ever-expanding crowd. People seemed to be coming from everywhere. He held up his hands, and the crowd quieted.

We're all unpaid actors in this play, said Langley to himself. He felt sick.

Alene and Joe Chechik stood right behind the attorney. Langley could see that every time a camera went off, Alene smiled. Langley knew this kid was worth a million bucks.

"I'm attorney Jack Mullaney." He was a talking legal head, a guy called in to comment on Lindsay Lohan trials and things like that. Langley shook his head. When he looked up he caught Bugbee's eye, and they both registered disgust on their faces.

Mullaney went through the whole sad story. How Alene was unhappy at home, how she felt confined by the Fahnestocks — "lovely people," he said — and how Alene wanted to "try to repair the damaged relationship with her father Joe."

This was important, too, you see, because Alene herself was interested in music and singing and a career in entertainment. She idolized her father and realized how important music was.

"Alene simply wanted to be with her father, and then, in the confusion that sometimes happen when families don't talk to each other as clearly as they should, things can sometimes get out of hand," Mullaney said.

There was nothing out of hand, thought Langley. There was nothing out of control. This thing was rolling along like clockwork. Just then his phone buzzed. It read, "private number," so Langley assumed it was Lucy Williams. He would call her back later.

Neither Alene or Joe would answer questions right now, said Mullaney. "Our first responsibility is to talk with the authorities who have been so concerned and diligent in searching for Alene." The first step in avoiding a criminal charge of theft of services, thought Langley, but everyone in this instance had played it smart. No one had done anything except the media.

Langley looked up to see if he could find Bugbee, but he had probably already gone into the room where they would question the missing persons.

Alene smiled for the cameras one more time. This kid was already famous, and she hadn't done a thing. Joe Chechik, a model of small-town, never-quite-made-it cool, remained expressionless. He was trying to convey the idea that all this attention was nothing new to him.

But Joe Chechik was going to take his fame any way he could get it, even if it meant blowing up his own family.

Nineteen

Thursday, May 9, 7:20 a.m., Ed Lustig's office. It was Alene on national TV a few days later who insisted none of this had been planned. "You have to understand, my father and I were trying to work things out, and we thought we could do it by ourselves."

She was good, Langley thought to himself. She was poised. The lines had been rehearsed, but she was putting them over. So good that she and Joseph Chechik were back appearing on *Today* with Jack Mullaney. Alene was asked what her plans were. Looking radiant and healthy and slightly dumbstruck, she said she wanted to have her own fashion line that she could launch on a reality TV show. She was also heading out to Los Angeles to cut a demo CD for a "big music producer."

Joey Cee, in an incredibly awkward moment, pulled out one of his own CDs and flashed it at the camera. His hair was thick and oily and black. And then he seemed to contradict his daughter about the whole thing not being staged.

"Oh, this was all art," he said with too much enthusiasm. "Everything is art! When you're rich and famous, you can make your own art. You're your own boss. You can do your own thing. You're free."

Free, Langley thought.

It was Catherine Fahnestock who first mentioned Langley Calhoun in public. She was on *Good Morning*

America and was questioned about the whole thing being fake, and Mrs. Fahnestock said, "We went to this private eye, Langley Calhoun, to help us find Alene."

"You went to a private eye?"

"He was famous," she said. "Everyone knew who he was. We knew he could get us the attention we needed."

"Do you mean attention for Alene and her career?" the host asked.

Catherine had let more out of the bag than she wanted to. You had to be practiced if you were going to lie in front of the media, and Catherine Fahnestock wasn't, so Jack Mullaney, sensing trouble, jumped in.

"No, the kind of attention we needed to find Alene," said the attorney.

Twenty

Friday, May 10, 10:15 a.m., Langley and Delia's house.
Britney Suwako of *The Fenton Herald* was one of many
reporters looking for a quote from Langley about the
incident. Langley told Britney the same thing he told every
other reporter, which was that he wasn't going to comment.

"Chief, I'm gonna need a quote. My story won't be
complete if I don't get a quote."

"I'm not going to say anything," said Langley.

"But you need to go on the record about this. It's a big
deal."

"You can say that I didn't want to comment. I don't
mind."

"Can I ask you why?"

"Sure."

"Come on, Chief, tell me why."

"Britney, enough."

There had been enough conversation about this in the
press already, Langley felt. "Why is it … " he started to
say, but he stopped.

"Why is it what, Chief?"

"This is off the record."

Britney sighed.

"I swear to God, Britney. I don't want to see one word
of anything I say in print. I don't want to see me quoted,
paraphrased, nothing. If you have to mention me, I can't

stop you, but don't speculate on anything about why I did what I did."

"Chief, I like you."

"You wouldn't know it by the book you wrote." Britney had published a true crime book about the crime involving his brother Brian that Langley had investigated. The book was called *A Modern Day Cain and Abel*, and in it Britney spilled out half-truths and innuendo about Langley's entire family.

"You can't blame me for making a little money."

"No, I can't blame you for that."

"And I mean very little money."

"You and me both," said Langley.

"So tell me why you want to be quiet about this? You should be proud."

"Proud?"

"Yes, proud."

Langley sighed.

"I'm just a reporter looking for a quote."

"Why do I have to say anything?"

Britney was quiet for a second. "We live in a time, Chief, when if people don't say anything about what they've done it seems as though they have something to hide."

"That's the world you created, not me."

"Not commenting is like bad air. There's something wrong about it."

"I'm beginning to think if I don't comment, you're going to write a column that asks people to wonder why I didn't say anything. Why I didn't talk, that there must be something wrong about my not saying anything. I can see that happening."

"I won't do that."

"You won't if I say something now, you mean."

"I didn't say that."

"Britney, you know what? I don't care. What I want to ... oh, nothing."

"What?"

"Nothing. Nothing. I mean it. Nothing."

"That's too bad, Chief."

"Write whatever you want."

"I have to now."

"The problem, Britney, is that you don't want a quote. What you want is permission."

"I don't need your permission."

"Permission to hurt me. If I participate in this, you're going to tell yourself you had nothing to do with the fallout. I'm a grown man, and if I somehow hurt my reputation or people get mad at me, then I should have known enough not to talk to you in the first place. So I do know enough, and I'm not talking to you. If you want to bust my balls in print, own it."

He hung up.

Twenty-One

Sunday, May 12, 1:00 p.m., Ed Lustig's office. Langley was looking around in his office, wondering if he should pack up or just let things be for a while. Ed Lustig came around the corner and stood in the doorway. It was the first time he had been in the office or seen Ed since the press conference in Hampton.

"You know some great people, Ed."

"We got the kid back. It all worked out."

Langley let out a heavy sigh.

"I didn't have any idea, you know," Ed looked at Langley, "that this was all a plot."

Langley stopped looking around for a second and smiled.

"No harm done," said Ed.

Langley was thinking about Delia. He was thinking about Brian. He was even thinking about Lucy Williams.

"What are you doing," Ed said, "packing? Are you leaving?"

"I don't know," said Langley, and he sat down in his chair.

"You've got a very troubled look on your face, my friend," said Ed.

Langley made a noise, a kind of grunt, to express his frustration.

"What is that noise?" said Lustig. "Jesus, man, speak English."

"No, nothing."

"Are you quitting?'

Langley sighed.

"Are you picketing?"

Langley shook his head. "I gotta go help out this woman I know back in town. She's sick."

"Okay."

Langley moved something on his desk.

"Okay," said Lustig. "You're pissed."

"Ed, really."

"Go help your friend."

"My friend," said Langley softly. "My friend."

Ed sat in the chair across from Langley. "Take a little time."

They both were quiet for a second. Lustig sighed. He took a cigarette out of a pack and put it in his mouth and lit it.

Langley waved the smoke away.

Twenty-Two

Thursday, May 23, 7:30 a.m., Fenton, NH. Langley was standing on his front stoop, newspaper in one hand and a coffee cup in the other, and he was watching the wind blow. It was blowing hard through the town, and the air was filled with pink and white blossoms that had blown off the trees. Little whirlwinds formed in the street, picking up the dust and the debris, and they scooted down the road like ghostly tops and then collapsed.

Delia was hanging laundry in the back yard, and the breeze carried with it the smell of their damp, clean sheets. He hadn't smelled that smell since he was a child, and he remembered his mother hanging sheets in the back yard on a string of nylon cord his father had stretched between two posts.

Langley closed his eyes and remembered, inch by inch, the topography of his back yard. The memory of the broken handle on his mother's wicker basket was clear.

"Hey," Delia said, "Whatcha doing?"

He smiled and looked at her. "You were up all night," he said.

"So were you," she said.

They stood looking at each other for a moment, but the winds and the early morning activity of the town were not enough to fill the silence between them. Langley had not done anything for a month. He was simply getting used to having Delia so close in his life. He looked at her. He hadn't called Ed Lustig, and he didn't call Lucy Williams.

"Is everything all right?" Delia had had a funny look on her face the past few days. She turned to him and put her arms around his neck and pushed her face onto his shoulder. Her face was warm and soft, and she kissed his shoulder, and she squeezed tight. Langley was completely uncertain about how to read what she was feeling. He did not want to ask again if she was all right, because by now he was afraid the answer was no, she was not all right, and the problem was him.

Delia breathed in deeply and then lifted her head and wrapped her fingers around the back of his neck. She looked at him with intent. She smiled, but then heavy, clear tears appeared in her eyes. They formed as if out of a deep fountain and they rolled gracefully down the cheeks of her beautiful face.

"I was just thinking that I might be pregnant," she said.
He looked up. His fingers started to tingle as he looked at her. He put his coffee cup and newspaper down. His feet were tingling, too. There were pins and needles shooting through his toes and up his leg, and he wanted to steady himself as he looked at Delia.

"I'm … I'm not really thinking I might be pregnant. I'm sure."

He drew her close to him, and he felt the warmth of her body, and he hoped she felt the same warmth from him. He breathed in and out, in and out. She was gently fingering the fabric of the polo shirt he had slept in.

"Oh, my God, honey," he said. "Oh, my God. I'm … " But then he grabbed her by her shoulders, leaned back and said, "How are you?

She nodded her head slowly. "I'm pretty good."

They both laughed lightly.

"We're going to have a baby," she said, and she was smiling. It was more than a smile.

Langley closed his eyes. He did not want to tell her how complicated his feelings were just then.

Delia wrapped her arms around his neck again. She was holding him firmly, and she kissed his neck over and over, and he pressed his hands on her back, and he did everything in his power not to fall over.

Twenty-Three

Saturday, June 8, 11:30 a.m., Fenton, NH. "Hey." Freddie Ouellette startled Langley. He had walked up behind and poked Langley on the shoulder.

"Hey buddy," said Langley happily. They shook hands.

"There she is," said Freddie.

They were both staring at a new bridge, or the beginnings of a new bridge, being built across the Oquossoc right at the bend where the width of the river was narrowest, maybe a little over one hundred feet. It was the bridge that Langley had seen the construction crew working on the day he was first at Lucy Williams' house. The old red covered bridge that had been in the exact same location, where Langley and others had fished for years, had been taken down whole and was now sitting about three hundred yards away in an open field on dry land.

Langley shook his head. "You know, when I went over to see Lucy Williams one day, I noticed the crew working on this, but I didn't think anything about it."

"Jake, it's Chinatown," said Freddie. Whenever Freddie thought something was corrupt, he quoted the last line of that Jack Nicholson movie. "I put a call in to Maria, but she hasn't returned my call." Maria Tull was the Chairman of the Board of Selectmen in Fenton. Freddie sneezed, and then he sneezed again. "Goddamn allergies," he said, as he wiped his nose. "When I left my house I saw a spiderweb that was covered in pollen. Can you imagine that?"

"What are they going to do with the old bridge?"

"Charlie said they were going to destroy it, but he wrote a letter to everybody asking for time to see if they could either sell it or get somebody to move it."

"Move it? Move it where?"

"I don't know," said Freddie.

Twenty-Four

Same day, noon. This was the part of town that had been Fenton's manufacturing center more than a hundred years ago. There had been mills along this part of the river, but they were all gone now. Town leaders in the 1960s, before gentrification was a word or a concept anyone knew about, decided in their wisdom to provide some short-term work to local construction companies by tearing down all the empty mills. The buildings weren't sleek and modern, so they had to go.

And they were all gone by 1970. When other towns along New Hampshire's Seacoast, like Portsmouth and Dover, started to see their old mills rehabilitated and bought and rented out in the early 1990s, Fenton didn't share in the economic boon.

All that was left were the scraps. This section of the river was lined with the granite stone walls that once were the foundations of the mills on the river's edge, and there was ancient debris in the river bed. The drum from an old combine lay there, and iron pipes of various lengths and sizes were strewn about just below the surface of the water. There was a chair of some kind flipped upside down and a bicycle. The bed of the river was covered with remnants of granite and brick from when the mills were built.

You could see all of that at low tide.

The Oquossoc cut through town from north to south and then bent eastward to empty into the Piscataqua. The developed part of town crept right up to the river's edge on the west side, the side where Langley and Freddie were standing. The road leading to the old bridge, Sandspit Road, came down through the Shoals where Lucy Williams and the Marabellas lived. But on the east side, the side the new bridge crossed over to, there was nothing, just an empty plot of land.

It was almost thirty acres of prime, undeveloped property. There were a couple of small municipal storage sheds on it, but the land sloped up to a young forest and then hit the border of nearby Dover. That part of the river was lined with weed trees and patches of land covered with high grass. Little paths cutting down to the river had been made by people who still fish in the Oquossoc.

Freddie reminded Langley that there had been a vote on building a new bridge twice at town meetings, and twice the people of Fenton had voted not to use town funds to build a new bridge.

But there it was.

"They're building this with money out of the contingency fund," said Freddie.

"Contingency fund?" Langley laughed.

"That's what I said," said Freddie.

"Who knew we had a contingency fund," said Langley.

"Except we don't anymore," said Freddie.

Langley and Freddie Ouellette had known each other for a long time. Langley had worked in the restaurant Freddie's family owned in York Beach up in Maine when he was a kid. He and Freddie had washed dishes and bussed tables and chased girls together. It was actually Freddie who chased the girls. Langley sat back and watched and laughed. Freddie owned the restaurant now.

"We tried to get a new ball field built, and the town said it didn't have the money. We tried to get the bike path built, and the town said we didn't have the money. We tried to get them to put in lights so the kids could use the skateboard park at night, and the goddamn town said we didn't have the money," said Freddie, who was divorced but had two kids he adored. "But all of a sudden we have money to build a new bridge right where the old bridge that works perfectly fine is?"

Freddie turned around and started to walk away from the river. "You want to know who's building this?" he asked as he walked away. He went behind the trailer that had been set up as the headquarters for the construction site. Langley followed.

Leaning up against the trailer was a big sign, supposedly made so it could advertise the project and the company in charge of it. It said, "The Oquossoc River Bridge Project. Brought to you by the People of Fenton, NH and the Todd S. Philbrick Construction Company."

"What do you think of that?"

"Todd Philbrick."

"That cocksucker," said Freddie, letting go of the sign so that it flopped on the ground face down. "You know what I remember about that guy? He never shuts up."

The two old friends flashed a glance at each other and smiled. Langley was remembering—and he knew Freddie was, too—about the time years ago when they were both at a Planning Board meeting that Todd Philbrick had spoken at. It was about a noise reduction ordinance, and Todd was supporting it, telling the board that Boston helicopters flew over his house all the time. "What do you mean, Boston helicopters?" asked the Chairman of the Planning Board.

"Because they sound like they're headed to Boston," Todd had said.

Langley sighed. He looked around and then back at the old, red, dry-docked bridge. Todd Philbrick was also a punk, a bully who was arrogant to the point of psychosis. He cheated on his tax bills, and he cheated on the basketball court. He cheated on his wife. He would have been tagged as a bully whether he lived in a small town or a big city. He was probably worse because he lived in a little town. He could throw his weight around, and there were fewer people to call him on it.

"How does a guy like Todd Philbrick keep getting ahead?" Langley asked.

"America rewards some strange people," Freddie said as he sighed. The two men stood silent for a moment. "I know you may not want to get your boots dirty again," said Freddie, "but you gotta help me start some kind of protest or something. We can't let this thing go through."

"The bridge is already started, Freddie."

"That isn't the point," said Freddie, lighting a cigarette. "First of all, there is no way the new bridge is going to look as nice as that old covered bridge. I don't think I want any of my tax dollars going to Todd Philbrick anyway. And the people who run this town can't just do what they want."

Langley thought this over for a minute. He shook his head. "I'm not interested in any kind of political thing, Freddie. I'm not …"

"This isn't any of that bullshit," said Freddie. "It isn't about that. You know me. Christ. I'm surprised you would even say that. I'm talking about I tried to get a playground built for my kids, and I couldn't, and we're wasting this kind of money. Your kid will need a place to play."

Langley then looked over at Lucy Williams' house. He was hoping he'd see her. His mind wandered back to her, and he was feeling guilty he hadn't called. He was using their pregnancy to avoid getting involved in other people's business, but the truth was he didn't want to face her sadness when he was feeling so undone himself.

"You ever hear anything about the river being polluted?" Langley said suddenly.

"What?"

"People getting sick here at the Shoals?"

"Sick?"

"Lucy Williams told me about it."

"Lucy Williams?"

Langley nodded.

"When did you talk to her?"

"She said the river was making her sick and had been making people sick for years. She said she's been trying to tell people about it."

"Today, these days?" said Freddie. "Are you thinking the new bridge has something to do with that?"

It was the furthest thing from his mind, but when Freddie said it, Langley just looked at him.

"She told me a little while ago she was dying, and she thought there was something in the water."

Langley and Freddie just stared out at the river.

"She thought something in the water made her sick?" said Freddie. "She's always been crazy, you know that."

Langley shrugged his shoulders, staring at the old covered bridge over there on dry land. He looked at the new construction and the dry, clay-like empty parcel. There was green all around the empty land. Suddenly the empty lot looked like it was scorched, unable to grow anything.

Then he looked at Lucy Williams' house, which was just a few hundred yards away, right up next to the river.

Twenty-Five

Monday, June 10, 10:30 a.m., Fenton, NH. Langley pulled into Lucy Williams' driveway and was walking up to the door when he saw Mrs. Marabella, the next door neighbor, coming toward him. He made a face, because he was sure that she was going to tell him something terrible.

"Lucy's in a coma," said Mrs. Marabella.

Langley blinked, but he didn't change his expression. "She — oh, Jesus," he said and looked up toward the sky.

"She's at Piscataqua Regional." Langley didn't say anything. "In Portsmouth." He knew where the hospital was. "Poor thing," added Mrs. Marabella, who was wearing a dull pink bathrobe.

Langley nodded and got back into his truck.

He pushed the button for the elevator and went up to the fourth floor. He shared the ride with a doctor who was wearing a tie that pictured dancing children. In Langley's experience, every time he met a teacher or pediatrician wearing a tie that seemed to celebrate children, he or she invariably turned out to be an asshole.

He walked down the hall. He hadn't been in that hospital in some time but was shocked by what he saw. There were patients on gurneys pushed up against the wall. There was equipment lining the hallways. It looked chaotic, cramped. This didn't look like a hospital in America.

He went into room 415 and heard a heavy industrial sound, then some gurgling. Lucy Williams' bowels were being emptied by a machine. The room was dull and impersonal. Langley shook his head. There were no cards, no balloons, no flowers, no nothing. The room was brown and indistinct. There were the efficient machines, a white board with her medication schedule on it, a curtain, a window that wouldn't open and a polished floor.

"Hello," said the nurse as he came into the room.

"Hello," said Langley. He watched the young man work for a moment and then asked: "What's happening? Can I ask?"

"Oh," said the nurse in a quiet voice, "she's comfortable. We're making her as comfortable as we can."

"I mean, ah," Langley cleared his throat. "Is there anything to be done?"

"And you are?"

"I'm a friend. I'm the former police chief in Fenton, Langley Calhoun."

"As I said, we're doing everything we can to make her comfortable, but I'm afraid that's all we can do at this point." The nurse's voice was quiet.

Langley listened to the push and pull of the machine, the pumping, gurgling, mechanical device that was performing a bodily function.

"She's going to die?"

The nurse walked over to Langley. "She's in her last stages, I'm afraid, yes."

"What happens when she dies?"

The nurse looked at Langley. "What happens?"

"What happens? She has no family. Who will attend to her? She doesn't have any family."

"Whoever is on duty, Mr. Calhoun. We won't neglect her. We'll take good care of her."

"No, I know." He sighed. He looked around the room. "Do you mind if I stay for a while?"

"No, not at all. She'll know you're here." Langley thought it was nice of him to say that. The nurse checked one more thing, then turned to Langley and said, "I'm very sorry."

Langley nodded. His mouth was set in a frown. He sat in a chair in the corner of the room.

He had planned to stay for only a little while, but he couldn't leave. He called Delia and told her where he was, and he stayed the night. He wondered if Lucy was dreaming, and what she was dreaming about.

It was a little after three o'clock in the morning when she died.

Twenty-Six

Tuesday, June 11, 3:20 a.m. It was a quiet death. Two people came in and looked at her, checked her vitals, then started switching off her life support. The moment when they draped her head with the sheet seemed so ancient to Langley that he was surprised they still did it.

No one said anything, but there was nothing really to say. When the attendant started to wheel her out of the room, Langley stood up. The young man turned around and looked at Langley.

"Do you want to say something to her?" The hospital was so empty his voice echoed.

"No," but there was a hesitation in his voice.

"Go ahead, it's okay."

Langley took a step forward and looked at the shape of her body under the blankets.

"Can I just see her face?"

The attendant nodded and pulled back the cover. Langley went over and looked at her and put his hand on her cheek. He was surprised that it had already become a little cool. Her mouth was slack, and the ropes of veins that had once defined her neck were now gone.

Langley nodded, and the man covered her again, and they went away. He looked around the room to see if he had brought a jacket with him, but he hadn't, and he walked out of room 415. He walked over to the desk.

"The woman who just died, Lucy Williams?"

The nurse looked up. "Yes?"

"Do you know who is listed as next of kin?"

"Are you her family?"

"No, I was the chief of police in the town we lived in, and we were friends."

She looked up the file in her computer. "The person listed is a Father Paul Kolker of St. Anne's Church in Kittery."

"Okay, thank you."

"Good night," said the nurse. "I'm sorry."

When Langley got home Delia was asleep. He shook her gently, and she opened her eyes. All he did was shake his head, and Delia knew that Lucy had died.

He called the church in the morning and explained to Father Kolker who he was, and he asked if there was anything he could do to help with the arrangements.

"Well, honestly, we have a fund, but Lucy wasn't a parishioner, and no one really knows her."

"How much do you need?" said Langley.

"Between the casket and the …"

"How much do you need?"

"I don't know."

"Buy the casket, take care of the funeral, and send me a bill," said Langley.

"I'm sorry to put this on you, Mr. Calhoun."

"It's not a problem. I'm happy to do it."

"Thank you, and God bless."

Twenty-Seven

Friday, June 14, 3:00 p.m., Bercovici Funeral Home. There weren't many cars in the parking lot. It was only fifteen minutes before the memorial service, and there was almost no one there. Langley looked over at Delia, who made a questioning face.

The death of Lucy Williams struck him hard. It was one of those strange connections sometimes people get with people they hardly even know. It's the kind of thing like when your favorite movie star dies, and you hardly bat an eyelash, but then someone more obscure, less well known, or that you'd barely ever heard of also passes away, and it affects you very deeply. It was like that for Langley with Lucy Williams.

Langley hated funerals, and he especially hated the funerals of young people. He didn't want to be there.

When they walked into the chapel at St. Anne's Church, Langley and Delia looked at each other. They were in the sanctuary, but there was no one there. Then they noticed a small sign that said "William's Service" — the name was misspelled — with an arrow. They followed the sign and ended up in what looked like a small parlor. It was dimly lighted, a calm, beige-colored room. Langley shook his head. They weren't going to have the service in the sanctuary because they weren't expecting many people.

There were six people in the room. Langley and Delia made eight. Langley saw two people who may have been friends with Lucy in school, a couple Langley knew, and two people who sat apart from each other. An older couple, who Langley recognized as the Marabellas, came in and sat in the back of the room without looking up at anyone.

"Christ," Langley whispered to Delia.

Chief Darrow came in, saw Langley and Deli, and came down and sat next to Delia. He shook their hands. Langley thought it was decent for the chief to show up. Going to funerals is not easy, even for people you do not know. Then Freddie Ouellette came in. He had given Langley some money to help with the funeral.

Lucy was lying in the open casket. Langley looked at Delia, who made the tiniest gesture with her face for him not to say anything.

Twenty-Eight

Same day, 3:30 p.m. Langley wondered what the priest was going to say. He was sure the eulogy was going to be a series of platitudes that could be applied to anyone, anywhere, because you did not know them.

They all sat, and a mild-looking young man stood before the tiny congregation with a Bible in his hand. Here we go, thought Langley, wondering briefly what his own funeral would be like. He was thinking of Danny's funeral, which had been attended by almost the entire town and had a punishing sadness to it.

"Welcome. Welcome, the family and friends of Lucy Williams. Welcome to this celebration of her life."

Celebration? Langley thought. Jesus.

As though he had read Langley's mind the priest added, "Her life was too brief, but during that time please know she was a woman who felt everything you have felt. Every joy, every bliss, every disappointment and every sorrow ... Lucy felt them all, and so her life was full in that way."

He paused. "I want those of you who knew her to take a moment to feel the spirit of this woman."

Langley looked over to see Lucy Williams' profile in the casket, and he imperceptibly nodded his head. He had seen Lucy Williams as many things, but not as a woman. He shook his head. He had not seen her as a woman.

"When I woke up this morning it was still dark, and I went into my little kitchen and made myself a cup of coffee, and I was looking out the window that faces the direction and location where the sun rises this time of year. I look out my window, and I can see the sky turn from black, with the streetlights still on, and watch as it gets imperceptibly lighter. Then I see streaks of color, bands of color, and this morning the sun came through the clouds, and I said to myself, it is going to be a beautiful day. And it is a beautiful day. We are here in sorrow, but it is a beautiful day. Of course, I realize that the warmth and light of the sun I feel now is heat and light that left the sun some time ago, but we still feel it. Think of Lucy Williams like that. She may have left us, but her heat and light will remain when we think of her."

He looked out over the small gathering. "The spirit of Lucy Williams is here before us, and it is our responsibility, if I may use that word, our responsibility to take the time to value her life. However slightly connected we all may have been while she was here, I am asking you to put some of your energy into recognizing her and remembering her, because she was a woman of worth and a woman who deserves our attention."

He gestured with the hand holding the Bible in the direction of the casket. "Lucy Williams is a woman created by God, a spirit of great worth," he said. "Think of her not only today but tomorrow. Think of her a year from now when you are driving in the car. Think of her not in sadness or remorse or regret, but think of her as a laughing, loving woman, and you will honor her life. Think of her that way, as an American woman who lived a full life, and she will live on as a person of worth. The love you have felt toward another human being can never be destroyed."

Langley looked up when he heard that. He looked over

at Delia. He thought of his brother Danny. Delia took her hand away and wiped her face.

"Every death is accompanied by many births, and each birth is the beginning of a great life. A good life. A serious life. And so when you are living your life, think of this woman."

The room was quiet. Chief Darrow had his head down. The crowd felt the weight of the simple task they had been asked to do.

"A great writer and thinker once said that the story of salvation is the story about men and women, about the burden and promise of being human."

Langley thought about how immediate and penetrating and devastating the death of someone can seem. Right after it has happened, it seems as though you're never going to get over it.

You think after someone dies you will never forget that person, but then over time, the presence fades, the voice is reduced to an echo, and you no longer feel the space he or she once took up. And then one day you wake up, and you realize ten years have gone by, and your life has changed, or it has not.

There is a woman, thought Langley, and he looked one last time at Lucy Williams, and then he looked at Delia.

Twenty-Nine

Later that same day. Chief Darrow handed Langley a cheap white cotton doctor's mask. "That bad?" said Langley.

"It's a shithole," said Darrow.

They were standing out in front of Lucy Williams' house. Some stuff was in the yard, chairs and table and boxes of books. There were boxes of dishes, bowls and plates. Langley looked in the boxes without touching anything. The dishes and the furniture were all covered with dust and dirt and mold from the rain and the wind.

The yard was unmowed, and it was dotted with ugly brownish toadstools that looked as if the tops had exploded.

Langley and the Chief went in through the back screen door. They weren't a foot inside the house when they were hit by a wall of stench, even though they were wearing masks.

The room was filled with piles of boxes. The walls were paneled, and there was a drop ceiling, but easily half of the panels in the ceiling had fallen out, and the wood and plumbing was exposed. There was a yellowed poster of Steve McQueen riding a motorcycle tacked up on the wall. He was jumping the barbed wire fence in *The Great Escape*. That must have belonged to Lucy's brother Ned.

To the right was a carpeted staircase. The carpet was filthy and almost worn through at the center of the steps. At the bottom of the stairs there was another open door, and that was an old room with the furnace and the washer and dryer. The room was draped with cobwebs. There were hanging cobwebs everywhere. Langley went over and saw a moldy load of laundry in the washing machine.

The door at the top of the stairs was closed. Langley took his mask off to test the air, but when he breathed in he realized the stench was unbearable. He put the mask back on and reached for a doorknob. When he touched it he pulled back because it had a gluey, gummy coating on it.

"Goddamnit," said Langley, and he wiped his fingers on his pants. For some reason an image of Delia's face flashed before him, and so against every instinct he had to keep going. He went back down the stairs and out through the back screen door, and he was out on the lawn once again.

He took off the mask and breathed in. He went to his car and squirted out some hand sanitizer and cleaned the funk off his fingers. He may have been holding his breath without even knowing it, because he was breathing hard and deep. He went back inside.

"I want to show you something," said Darrow at the top of the stairs.

As they walked through the house Langley realized he was in a house so foul and disgusting, it was no wonder Lucy Williams was sick. There was a thick coating of yellow dust covering almost everything. It looked like pollen, but Langley knew it wasn't. It was dust, and he remembered a fact, which may have been true and may not have been, that house dust was actually dried up human skin.

There was an old vacuum cleaner in the living room, but when Langley squeezed the bag it was flaccid and empty. No one had done any cleaning in here for a long time.

"This must have been Lucy's room," the Chief said. He walked through the open door. Langley saw a nice old king-sized bed covered with a yellow quilt. The room was neater than any other room in the house, and there were pictures of Lucy and her family on the wall. There was even an old picture with Langley in it from the time they all had driven to Lake Winnepesaukee one summer, the Williamses and the Calhouns, in an attempt to see if the parents could be friends. It never worked out that way, but Langley remembered that it had been a nice day.

There was an old-style desktop computer sitting on a desk. Langley went over and looked at the keyboard, which was dirty, but it wasn't covered with dust. He thought Lucy must have used it regularly. Tacked up on the wall was a pink construction paper heart, like the kind you would get in grammar school, with the words "Love you" printed on it.

Langley switched the computer on, and the screen saver soon popped up, a picture of the Oquossoc river in the summertime. He clicked on the Google Chrome icon. The Google search home page popped up, and Langley clicked on the gmail link. He couldn't get into Lucy's account, if she even had one, and then Chief Darrow came into the room.

"Hey, Chief," said Langley, tapping the computer. "Can you impound this? Can we check the hard drive?"

"What are you thinking about?"

"I don't know. Her email, maybe. Anything about what she was thinking, who she was talking to."

"Sure," said Darrow, "but take a look at this." He leaned over and opened up a cardboard box and lifted out a Ball jar that was half-filled with a clear liquid. A piece of masking tape had been attached to the side of the glass, and it said, "Oquossoc water, May 15." He handed the jar to Langley and then pulled out another. It was labeled "Oquossoc water. May 22." The Chief put down the jar and walked over to another door. He opened it, and in the room beyond there were perhaps a dozen moving boxes piled high, each filled with samples of water from the Oquossoc River.

Langley went over and picked out a jar. He lifted it up to the light and looked at the water. It looked clear and clean.

Thirty

Outside Lucy Williams' house. Chief Darrow blew out a long white plume of cigar smoke. They were standing out in the back yard, holding their masks in their hands.

Langley smelled the cuff of his shirt. "Jesus Christ," he said. He wanted to get out of those clothes immediately and burn them.

"She told you the river was making her sick?"

"She thought the water had given her cancer. She was concerned that people all over the neighborhood might get sick."

"She was keeping that water for some reason." Langley fell silent.

"Lucy Williams left no will," said the Chief out of the blue. Langley could feel his clothes start to curdle on his skin. "I'm not sure the house can be saved. We had the health inspector in here. It's bad."

Langley looked up at the dirty and broken windows. "Do you mind if I take a few of those jars?" he asked.

Darrow shook his head, silently indicating he didn't mind. "Just let me know what you take." He got into his car.

Langley went back into the house. He took a box of jars full of water and brought them out to his truck.

Thirty-One

Tuesday, June 18, 12:15 p.m., Ed Lustig's office. Langley had been given a key to Ed Lustig's office a long time ago, but if they happened to arrive at the same time, he always let Lustig open the door first. It was still Ed's office, it still had his name on the door. Langley had never asked, nor would he, to put his name on the sign. He was better known than Ed, and Langley's association with Ed had brought Ed some business, but Langley still figured it would have been rude to ask Ed for an equal partnership. He didn't want it, anyway.

So when they arrived at the office at the same time that morning, he let Ed open the door. Langley was spending time at the office because Delia told him to get out of the house and do something, but there really wasn't any work.

He went into his office down the hall, put his keys down, opened up his Dunkin' Donuts bag and took out his coffee and donut. He took the lid off the coffee cup and watched the steam rise. He dipped the donut into the coffee, took a bite and turned on his computer. He didn't even wait for it to boot up before he walked down the hall to Ed's office.

He set the cup down on Ed's desk. Ed had turned on his computer, and he watched the screen light up. He had an old black and white picture of the actress Gena Rowlands as his screen saver.

"What's up?"

"You know Lucy Williams claimed that there was something wrong with the environment, that something was making her sick?"

"Uh huh."

"I was in her house the other day. Darrow asked me to go. The house …"

"Who's Darrow?"

"He's the new chief in Fenton."

Lustig nodded.

"The house was probably the filthiest place I had ever been in. Not just cluttered, but filthy, and I've been in some houses that would make your skin crawl."

"I bet."

"She had kept jars and jars, boxes full of jars, filled with samples of water from the Oquossoc River which ran right by her house."

Lustig looked up. "She was keeping them? For what?"

"Evidence, I think. She told me the river was making her sick. I took some with me."

Ed thought for a moment. "She never said a word to you about them when you met?"

"Darrow found them when we went through her house."

"So she was collecting samples as evidence the water was making her sick."

"I'm guessing."

"And you don't know if she ever had them tested."

"She didn't say anything to me about them."

"You're never going to get anywhere with those samples. Any lawyer, a bad lawyer, would demolish that in court, never mind a good one. You don't even know where they really came from, if that's what you're asking."

"That's what I'm asking."

"But you should have them tested. They could tell you something."

Langley looked down.

"What?" said Lustig.

"I swam in that river every summer all summer. All the kids did." Langley paused. "There were tanning mills all along it decades ago. We'd always heard that it was so filthy back in the fifties and sixties, but by the time we came along everyone said it was okay to swim in it, although people didn't fish out of it. Not until recently."

"So the river is healthier."

"Everyone thought so."

"Okay," said Lustig.

"I'm just saying that maybe she had a good reason to believe her environment was killing her."

"Well, if that's the case, then anyone who swam in that river, including you, has the potential to get sick, I guess is what you're saying."

Thirty-Two

Wednesday, June 19, 9:30 a.m., Fenton, NH. The next morning Langley called the Marabellas and asked if he could stop by and ask them a few questions about Lucy Williams and the river. It was Mr. Marabella who picked up the phone. He hesitated, but Langley heard his wife say in the background, "What the hell difference does it make?"

When Langley arrived he was brought through the kitchen. In the corner of the room was a stack of unused packing boxes. There was also a pile of newspapers. He looked around. It was hard to determine whether they were getting ready to pack up and leave or those things had been sitting there for some time.

Mrs. Marabella asked Langley to wait in what she called the sunroom. She was dressed in a drab bathrobe. It was ten o'clock in the morning, and she hadn't gotten dressed yet. She looked like one of those people who have nothing to look forward to day after day and long ago stopped caring what they looked like. Her white roots were showing, and she pulled her robe up close to her neck in a gesture of demureness that seemed completely out of keeping with the setting.

Langley expected her to ask him if he wanted a cup of coffee, but she simply looked at him and frowned. She had bags under her eyes. Langley felt bad for her. It didn't seem as if she could be more than sixty or so, and yet he definitely had the feeling life was over for her. No joy, no sex, no aspirations — maybe too few good memories.

Langley went into the sunroom. To get in he pushed back two sliding wooden doors. They slid into the walls, and Langley couldn't remember seeing doors like that in a Fenton home before. The room was bathed in morning light. He could see why they called it the sunroom.

The walls were covered with bookshelves, and he read the titles. There were how-to-get-rich books, how-to-build-your-self-esteem titles, and books on the occult and the afterlife. There were dozens of books on how to be a better person. There were anger management books, guides to better living, books on how to organize your life and how to be a good corporate manager.

He thought perhaps they were both holding on by a thread. He also wondered if they were at all self-conscious about Langley seeing their library or if they led such insular lives they didn't think the world was looking at them at all anymore.

Mr. Marabella came into the room, and now that he was alone with him, Langley tried not to let on he still didn't like him.

The man before him seemed angry, pinched. He wore a Christian cross around his neck on a thin gold chain. His hair was long, curly and gray. His shirt was open at the collar.

Langley could see that Marabella had once been a sensualist; he didn't deny himself anything, whether it was drink or food and probably, over the years, women. He suddenly wondered what horrors Marabella had inflicted on his wife because of his infidelities, his indifference, his casual cruelties. Langley had seen these guys before, whether they were young or old, and they were always in a crisis. Their money ebbed and flowed, their looks waned, their bodies began to betray them. And then they lashed out even more.

"Would you care to sit, Chief?"

"I appreciate your taking the time to see me."

"Well, we felt somewhat ... paternal toward Lucy, as you can imagine."

"She had asked me to consider looking into whether there was any reason … well, she thought the Oquossoc was poisoned and making her sick."

"I've been around here a long time," said Marabella. Langley thought he seemed softer now, more human, than what he remembered as a kid. "Lucy seemed so helpless for most of her life." He shook his head. "I used to see her out in the yard. She was always sick, Chief, even as a child."

"You both have had cancer, correct? You and Mrs. Marabella?"

"Yes. Mine was melanoma, though, so it wasn't anything about the water. My wife had bladder cancer."

"You're both healthy now?"

"Oh, yes, that seems to be in the past. We feel fine." There was a pause.

"I understand," Langley said.

"Lucy was delusional, you know, at the end.

"I saw her," said Langley.

"I know."

"Yes. She didn't seem delusional at all."

"Well, I mean, did you see her house?"

"I did."

"What did that tell you?"

"It told me that she was tired and sick."

"Well." Marabella sat back in his chair and put his hands on his knees. "We never talked about the river, Chief. She never said anything to us."

"Are you planning on moving?"

"No."

"You've brought out some packing boxes and paper."

"You get a little older, Mr. Calhoun, you don't want to dust any more, clean so many things. Sometimes you just have to let go of the past. So we may be … divesting, but we're not moving. At least we have no plans to today."

Langley stood. "Thank you for your time." He extended his hand. "If you ever think of anything that Lucy may have said, or any other neighbor, for that matter, please let me know." He handed Marabella his card.

"Will do."

When he walked through the kitchen again, Langley noticed a water cooler with a half-empty five-gallon container on the top.

Thirty-Three

Sunday, June 30, 7:45 a.m., Langley and Delia's house.
Langley was thinking it was time to mow the lawn. The dandelions had taken over, and the little patch of grass, split in half by a short concrete walkway to the front door, had a decidedly weedy, unshaven look. He was thinking he'd buy a few of those miniature flags to line his walkway to celebrate the Fourth of July.

He had been preoccupied because Delia seemed somewhat distant, and as he was looking at his lawn he decided he was simply going to ask her about it. He knew it had something to do with the baby. He found her in the kitchen, and she was swinging what looked like a toy tennis racket in her hand. "What's that?" he said.

"It's a portable bug zapper." Delia handed it to him.

"You mean like a regular bug zapper?"

"Push the button on the handle, and when you see a horsefly you swat it like a tennis ball and *zap*." He made a face and handed it back to her. He looked at her, and she looked at him.

"Honey," she said. "I want to go to the doctor." She said it so quickly it startled him.

His knees almost buckled. "What's wrong?"

"I don't know, I don't know. I feel worried, but it's more than that," she said.

"We'll make an appointment right away," Langley said.

Delia never felt anxious. He trusted her feelings.

Thirty-Four

Wednesday, July 3, 10:00 a.m., Dr. Zolmian's office, Durham, NH. Among other things, Dr. Zolmian ordered another screening for Down Syndrome. He had done it at the beginning of her pregnancy as part of the routine, and the test had come back negative, but now he was doing it again.

"We'll find out if anything is going on," said the doctor. "There's nothing to worry about."

Nothing to worry about, thought Langley. What an utterly useless phrase. Nothing to worry about when a doctor is ordering tests and has a cloud passing over his face. Goddamnit, I don't want anything to be wrong.

It would be a few days before the results were in. Dr. Zolmian said he would call her. They drove home, and Delia looked out the window.

"Waiting is the worst part," said Langley. Delia looked over, and the expression on her face frightened him.

When Dr. Zolmian did call, he asked them to come into the office. They sat in chairs placed in front of his desk in a pattern that almost seemed designed to convey bad news. The air in the room was stale. The doctor's expression was unhappy. Langley looked at Delia and lifted his eyebrows and frowned.

"Okay," said Delia.

They squeezed each other hands. The doctor opened his mouth and started to speak, and the words sounded as though they were coming through water. The baby was healthy, but tests had shown the baby had Down Syndrome.

"The baby is healthy?" Delia said. "What?"

"Yes, perfectly healthy. Everything is, um, working as it should." The doctor's voice was steady, but his steady, calm tone annoyed Langley. It was at this point that he wanted some emotion. He wanted something in the doctor's voice to tell him everything was either going to be a disaster or was going to work out fine.

"The test is correct?" Delia asked.

The doctor nodded his head, and it was then Delia started to cry. The doctor had a box of tissues on his desk, no doubt just for moments like this, and a stream of tears fell down Delia's face.

Langley put his hands through his hair and wanted to jump up and out of the room. He wanted to unleash a torrent of curses.

"This condition does not necessarily present any ... undue ... complications for the pregnancy."

Langley stood up. Jesus Christ, he said to himself. He didn't mean to turn his back on Delia, but he did.

"Down Syndrome babies are almost always very happy, very content people," the doctor said, and Langley looked at the ceiling. "We'll keep a close eye on you and the child," said Dr. Zolmian.

"Yes, of course," said Delia, but her voice had never sounded so weak.

"I want to give you a little time to absorb this," said the doctor.

"Yes, of course," said Delia again, wiping her eyes.

The doctor said he needed to see his next patient, but Delia and Langley were welcome to sit in the office for as long as they needed. "I know it's a lot to absorb," he said. He stood and made a motion to shake Langley's hand as he passed, but it was a half-hearted gesture, and Langley wasn't going to respond anyway.

The doctor left, and the two of them were alone in the room.

Thirty-Five

Later that same day. Delia curled up on her bed, clutching a pillow, tears streaming down her face, shouting, "Stupid! Stupid! Stupid! Stupid!" She had been questioning everything she had ever done, every drug she'd taken, every beer she'd drunk. Why had she spent so many years doing yoga, eating properly? Why? What good had any of it done? Her anger at herself was frightening.

Langley sat in the chair. Everything about her body indicated she didn't want to be touched or comforted. It hadn't mattered that Dr. Zolmian said it wasn't the result of anything either of them had done, it was just that statistically the odds of having a child with Down Syndrome improved when the birth mother was older.

"Improved?"

"It was just a manner of speaking," said the doctor, but at that moment, Langley knew, Delia hated him. She had been going to that doctor for fifteen years.

Later, when she was asleep, Langley put a blanket over her and discovered that she was lying on top of some flyers and other papers about special needs children Zolmian had given her. He pulled the crushed papers out from underneath her and put them on the night table next to their bed.

Langley went into the kitchen and poured himself a glass of wine and stared out the window. It was a sultry summer night. The air was heavy and wet, and the leaves of the trees hung low as though they were slightly defeated by the heat.

Thirty-Six

Thursday, July 4, 5:00 p.m., Tim Calhoun's home, Fenton.
"The doctor thinks the baby has Down Syndrome." Langley and Delia were sitting in his father's living room. Tim Calhoun, Langley's father, looked at them both and then sat down in the chair next to Delia. His eyes grew dark and cold for a moment as he processed the news, shaking his head almost imperceptibly. Tim's girlfriend Vance put her hands over her eyes.

"How are you?" Tim asked Delia.

"Not good," she said.

"How're you?" he said to his son. Langley just made a face and shrugged his shoulders. "Are you two strong enough for this?"

Langley looked at his father. "We haven't even … I mean, we don't even know what it means," said Langley.

"It means you'll have the baby, and we'll get through it," Vance said. She was drying her eyes. "I'm sorry," she said. "I shouldn't have said that."

"Don't be sorry," said Delia, and that made Vance cry even more. Delia went over and sat next to her.

"What did the doctor say?"

"Just that this was what was happening, and it wasn't all that unusual, in a way."

"This child will be so loved," said Vance.

There was silence. Suddenly Tim Calhoun looked a little concerned. "You're not, you're not …?" He couldn't even say the word abortion. The old man was not religious, and he had never forced his kids into going to church, but he was also almost seventy years old and had been brought up Catholic, so it was something that didn't sit well with him. Langley was sure of that.

"Dad, we're not even thinking anything. Don't get nervous."

"I think we just need a little time to soak all this in," said Delia.

His father took a deep breath. "Okay," he said.

Thirty-Seven

Tuesday, July 9, 5:00 p.m., Antonio Meli's house, Fenton.
"Chief?" Antonio Meli still called Langley Chief, partly out of respect and partly out of mischief. They were on the phone, and Langley asked Antonio if he could come by.

Langley had known Antonio a long time, and in the past few years they had grown so close that Antonio, who was eighty-three years old, had entrusted Langley and Delia with the care of his property after he died. He had turned it into a land sanctuary, and he'd asked the two to live there and take care of the land and the animals on it so that it would never be developed. Langley truly loved the old man.

The sky that day was an almost unbroken canopy of pale blue. There was one cloud straight in front of Langley. It was thin and curved, but it didn't look as if it was hanging in the sky. It was rather like a slit leading to someplace far deeper behind the wide blue canvas.

"How's my girlfriend?" Antonio asked about Delia when they were standing in his kitchen drinking an afternoon Black and Tan.

Langley sighed. "We're going to have a baby."

Antonio walked over to Langley and hugged him and patted him on the back. He kissed him on the cheek.

"Good man," said Antonio.

"There may be a complication," said Langley, and the

smile went from Antonio's face. "The baby may have Down Syndrome."

Antonio thought for a moment. "Baby healthy otherwise?"

"Seems to be."

"Well, you're going to live here," Antonio said robustly. "You'll have your own society among the birds and the bees." Antonio poured Langley a glass of beer and handed it to him.

Langley thought about that phrase for a second, "the birds and the bees," and he wondered if his child would ever have that kind of relationship, be loved like that.

"Everything is going to be fine," said Antonio.

"I wanted to ask you something," said Langley, "Didn't you have someone come out here and check your well last year?"

"Dr. Schumann. She's a chemist." Antonio put his glass down on the counter. "I called her up a year or so ago because I thought all that dumping going on back there might have contaminated my well."

A landfill had once operated behind Antonio's house and had been at the center of the business between Brian and Langley a couple of years ago. The owner of the landfill had been involved in illegal animal trafficking and money laundering, and Brian, who was the attorney for the landfill owner, had covered up for him. With the help of Antonio Langley found out about it, and Brian and a few others, including the owner of the landfill, went to jail.

The whole thing started because Antonio had found a decapitated rare eagle on his property, and he thought the owners of the landfill were trying to frighten him. That one little bird unraveled the whole thing.

"How were the tests on the well?"

"Fine, but I asked her to come out here every two months to test it to make sure. So far so good, but of course, they've stopped dumping back there."

"How did you find out about her?"

"I called up the University. They found her for me."

"At NHU?"

"Yup. What's all this about?"

Langley took a sip out of his glass. "I may need to ask her something." Langley told Antonio the story about Lucy Williams and what she'd said about the river.

"Dr. Schumann can test that water for you," said Antonio, "tell you what's in it." But then he made a face.

"What?" said Langley.

"People find out you think that river is still polluted, you'll raise a shitstorm."

"I know," said Langley.

"There are plans to develop that property. It's worth millions but not if there's something wrong with the water."

Langley nodded and put his glass down. "What's the name of the chemist again?"

"Dr. Schumann. I have her number." Antonio picked up his phone and then put it down again. "Hold on." He left the room and came back with a book in his hands. "I got this at a lecture she gave over at the science center."

He handed the book to Langley. It was called *Betaphysics*, written by Dr. Willa Schumann, and had a fanciful image on the cover. The earth was held in a giant drop of water, and the drop was filled with tiny images of all kinds of wildlife and plants and animals, plus an image of two people that Langley had the distinct impression were Adam and Eve.

"Did you read this?" he asked Antonio.

"I did. Strange, but I liked it. We're all creatures from another planet, brought here by an interplanetary rainfall." Antonio laughed and shook his head. "She has this theory about why looking at a body of water calms us down."

Langley thought of all the walks he took at the beach or down by the Oquossoc.

"It's because we're made of water, mostly. Water is us." Antonio looked at Langley. After a moment he said, "You're not looking for some connection between the river and the condition of your baby?"

"I'm just trying to follow through on a promise I made Lucy Williams," Langley said.

Thirty-Eight

Thursday, July 11, 2:45 p.m., New Hampshire University.
"Dr. Schumann?"

Langley was sticking his head into a small office on the bottom floor of a building over at New Hampshire University. He was holding one of the Mason jars he had taken from Lucy Williams' house.

She stood and shook Langley's hand. "Mr. Calhoun," she said.

"Thanks for taking the time to meet with me." He went into her office. He had called a few days earlier and explained briefly what had happened to Lucy and about the water samples they had found in her house.

"I didn't make the connection at first," said Schumann, looking at Langley. "You're the police officer who was on the news, with the eagle, a couple of years ago."

"That was me, yes," said Langley.

"Your brother was involved?"

"Yes."

There was a slight pause. "I'm sorry," she said.

Langley's unease must have been apparent, because Schumann simply dropped the subject. Langley tried not to think about it. He still hadn't read the letter Brian had mailed last winter.

The professor held out her hands for the Mason jar, which Langley handed over. She held it up to the light and shook it. She then read the date on the masking tape on the outside of the glass.

"How many did you say there were of these?"

"Dozens."

Schumann lifted her eyebrows. "If her determination were indicative of a fact, then perhaps we could say that she was right, the river is polluted," she said. "She was determined."

"Can you test them?"

"Sure, but if you're looking for something like evidence, as proof, one sample just isn't going to do it."

"Is it possible that, ah, if she swam in the river as a child, if she swam and swallowed the water, and it got into her skin, the water would make her sick or even have some kind of effect years later? Is that possible?" Langley had a knot in his stomach.

"It wouldn't be the water that made her sick, Mr. Calhoun," Schumann said, putting the jar on her desk. "It would be what we put in it."

"She said no one believed her that the river — the, ah, pollutants — were making her sick." Langley mentioned the instances of cancer in the area. "I'm not sure she was ever stable, even as a kid, but this idea was clearly driving her to paranoia, I'd guess you'd call it."

"Of course the pollutants could make people sick, Mr. Calhoun. The idea is to try to get people to recognize it, which is very hard to do. If somebody dumped something in the river, and it was proved, then somebody would have to pay. But the companies that operated along the river were closed a long time ago. Who can be held accountable?"

"I don't know."

"I'll test it. We'll see." She looked at the water in the jar.

"The woman, the woman who was sick, was a friend of yours?"

"She came to me for help."

"I'd like some recent samples from the river, too," Dr. Schumann said. "Can you do that?"

"I can do that," said Langley.

Thirty-Nine

Sunday, July 14, 11:30 a.m., Portsmouth, NH. Dr. Zolmian had on a golf shirt and jeans and Langley thought he looked like a regular guy. In this context that was not a compliment. Outside his physician's office he looked bereft of authority and esteem and knowledge. He looked like a guy waiting in line for a cup of coffee.

Langley and Delia were sitting at a small round table, looking at an uneaten muffin and bagel, sipping their coffee, looking at each other. They were there to talk to Dr. Zolmian about the baby.

Delia had asked Langley to take her out for a cup of coffee, and on the way there she told him Dr. Zolmian was going to meet them. "We're going to talk about what we're afraid of, what you're afraid of," she said, "and I want you to say it out loud."

Dr. Zolmian came over to the table and sat down. He had a silver chain around his neck. Langley had never realized Dr. Zolmian had a mustache. His commitment to observation, something he'd always been aware of when he was a cop, was waning.

"So," Dr. Zolmian said and smiled. He turned his coffee cup in his fingers. He was nervous, too. There was a slight pause. "How are you two doing?"

Delia hunched her shoulders. "We're okay," she said. "It's rough."

"I understand … well, no," the doctor replied and

smiled again. "I don't understand anything. I can appreciate your concern."

"We're just ... we just want to make sure we're making the right decision," said Delia.

Zolmian looked up. "Have you decided on something? We can't really wait any longer if you choose to terminate."

"No." Delia paused. "We want to make sure whatever we decide is right."

"Are you thinking one way or the other?"

"Yes," said Delia. "We're going to have the baby." Zolmian sat back. "I want to have the baby. I want to, but I can't get my husband ..." She looked at Langley and smiled. "I can't get an answer out of Langley."

Dr. Zolmian didn't say anything. They were surrounded by the everyday noises of a coffee shop. There was low chatter, the ringing of the cash register, footsteps and the louder voices of people greeting each other. But their table seemed to be ringed in darkness.

"What are your concerns?"

Delia looked at Langley. "You have to talk about what you're feeling, honey." Langley didn't say anything. "Honey?"

"Let me ask you a question." Dr. Zolmian took a sip of his coffee. "Is there anything at all, and I mean this sincerely for both of you, I guess, but Delia, I've known you a long time, and I'm not really worried about you. So maybe this is for you, Langley. Is there anything in you that makes you think you'll be embarrassed about your child or, given the struggles the baby will have, you'll resent having it or resent Delia for having it?" He took another sip. "Do you think you won't be able to see it through?"

"See it through?"

"See the pregnancy through, the birth, the life of the child. See it through to the day you die." Langley looked at the doctor. "Because it's the men who cut out. The mother will protect that child fiercely, she will do what she needs to do for the child. But the men ..."

Langley took in a deep breath.

"The worst is the men who start well and then collapse and leave. That's the worst for everybody." Dr. Zolmian took a sip of coffee. "Delia has told me you have two children from a previous marriage that you don't see."

Feelings of shame and remorse poured through Langley's mind and body. He suddenly felt himself go weak. That had hurt, but it was true. He couldn't deny its truth. But it hurt.

"I can't counsel you about what to do. I won't, and I can't. I believe in choice, just so we're clear, but I have never guided anyone in that direction because the choice is so much more than simply aborting a fetus. I have seen couples fall apart after they have had a special needs child, and I almost wished I had counseled them not to have it, because I see the child go up for adoption, and then the adoptive parents can't handle it, and the kid ends up in foster care, going from home to home." He stopped. "So. If you won't be able to see it through, then that is what you two need to talk about."

Langley's first reaction was to become defensive. But he looked at Delia, and she was looking at him with care and concern, and he knew he would be a fool if he didn't realize she was right to be concerned.

The table was quiet, and Delia sat back in her chair and folded her arms across her chest. Even if he had become less observant, he could tell she was fed up with his inability to be clear about his feelings.

"He's worried because his brother is in jail, and he feels guilty about that. He had a woman he was trying to help die on him," Delia said. "He was blamed for another brother's death. He carries with him all this guilt."

Langley did not like having his life reduced to a series of disasters. He didn't like the way it made him feel confused and as though things were out of control, but when Delia said it, he also knew that was the way things were.

What Delia didn't know was that she had gotten the root of Langley's fear wrong. His basic fear was that the baby would die before him, and he wondered if that happened, would he die himself?

"I am afraid," Langley said, his voice hoarse and choked, and Delia reached out in alarm and grabbed his hand. He cleared his throat. Zolmian nodded. "I read that these babies only live to be about twenty."

Dr. Zolmian nodded again.

"I'm afraid I would always be thinking of that day when the child dies and not enjoying what … you know, what was happening right at that moment." He let out a deep breath.

"I can understand that," and Zolmian was looking at Delia when he said it. "I can only recommend counseling for you to learn how to deal with that."

Delia was squeezing Langley's hand. "I'm afraid of children dying," said Langley. He was thinking of the day his brother had fallen out of a tree.

"If you choose, and I mean the two of you and your families, if you choose for the baby to have a great life, then the baby will have a great life, and you will, too, no matter how long the child lives." They all breathed a little sigh of relief and exhaustion.

"I want them to be safe. They won't be victims of my ... bad luck." That's what Langley had thought for all those years. His voice was hoarse and quiet, and Delia was gripping his hands. "If I had to be honest, I was ... relieved when Julie took the kids away, when they went to Pennsylvania. I knew they wouldn't be victims of my bad luck."

Langley remembered the silence that had surrounded his own house when he was a kid after Danny died. There was a lot of activity at first, people stopping by and bringing meals, people he knew, people he didn't know. But then it all drifted away, and he remembered the image of his mother sitting at the kitchen table, weary and troubled, smoking cigarette after cigarette and lightly hugging Brian or Langley as they went through the kitchen. Langley remembered how thin she got, her arms withered up, and she seemed never to recover fully.

Their father would go down to the VFW hall and drink the early evening away, then come home surly and silent. There had been too much silence in that house for too many years, and so the quiet he heard now was unsettling.

There are no rules when a child dies. If a child dies, then there is no reason why everything else can't fall apart. Langley had felt that way since Danny died, and he was exhausted by the thought of it. He didn't want to feel that way anymore. He wanted to sleep through the night now. He didn't want to hear Danny's screams, or anybody else's screams, anymore. He didn't want his new baby to be lonely and wanting.

Then he remembered, or rather he couldn't forget, the silence in his own house years later between Julia and him, and the girls and the ticking of the clock and the dripping of the faucet. He thought of all those times he had driven by his parents' house and sat out front. He didn't know what he was looking for.

He did know, though, and what he was looking for was impossible to find. He wanted to drive up to his parents' house and turn in the driveway and be greeted by Danny and his mother and father and Brian. He wanted their voices to be happy, and he wanted to hear the sound of the basketball bouncing on the driveway, the bounce with the little ping in it when the ball was full of air, and he wanted to hear the insults and the banter and the laughter as they all played together.

He had this idea that all he had to do was turn into that driveway, and it would be all right, everything would be all right. But he sat in the coffee shop now and wondered why he longed for that, because he had the power and the ability to have it with Delia. It was right in his own hands if he wanted it.

He looked at her and realized how tired his eyes were. He could feel the strain behind them, and he held her hand. "I, um," he said and shook his head.

"If you're going to say something that will make me unhappy, I don't know if I want to hear it."

He looked up at the ceiling. He told her how he used to want to turn into the driveway of his parents' house and have everything be the same as it was when he was young.

"I just wanted to get back to the time when we were happy, you know, and for a long time I thought the only thing that could make me happy was if me and Danny and Brian were together again."

Delia started to cry. Langley put a hand over his mouth for a moment before continuing. "There was nothing else but that. Not you, not Julia, not Patty or Nancy, nothing, nobody except Danny and Brian and my mom all being in that house."

Delia's hands were clasped together, and her knuckles were white.

"So I stopped driving by the house, stopped that stupid wish … "

"It wasn't stupid."

"… and I figured that was just the way it was going to be. Everything would always be shit, and there was nothing I could ever do that would make me happy ever again."

They were silent.

"But now," he cleared his throat. "But now when I turn into our driveway, when I see your car parked there, I do feel happy, and I'm afraid of anything that could take it away from me."

"Oh, my darling," Delia said.

He was in anguish. "I'm terrified Patty or Nancy or … our baby is going to die." He put his head in his hands. "I need to be forgiven."

"Oh, honey, no, no, no, no, no. You don't need to be forgiven."

Langley looked at the doctor and Delia. He had let her down. They had finally gotten together, finally fallen in love. They were two people who might have been lucky enough to really be in love, not only love each other but like each other, and despite that, the two of them, the combination of their genes, had resulted in this happening.

"Ahh, I just don't know," he said.

Forty

Tuesday, July 16, 8:30 a.m., Fenton, NH. It was 9 o'clock at night, and Freddie Ouellette and Langley were lying on their stomachs on a concrete apron that lined a small section of the Oquossoc River. The air was filled with the sounds of cicadas and crickets. Freddie and Langley had had a few drinks, and they were lowering a jar tied to a string down into the water of the Oquossoc to get a fresh sample. They wanted to get some water from the deep part of the river, right where it made its big turn before Watchmen's Mill and the location of the new bridge.

They were lifting the filled jar out of the water when a flashlight popped on.

"Hey, hey, hey!" said a voice behind Langley and Freddie. "That's a mistake."

They twisted around, both still on their stomachs, and saw Todd Philbrick walking briskly toward them. Freddie and Langley looked at each other and grimaced.

"What are you doing there, guys?"

Langley finished lifting the jar with the string that he had tied around the lip of the jar. He screwed the top onto the jam jar and wrapped the string around the outside. He and Freddie scrambled to their feet.

"Looks like you boys had a little too much to drink," said Todd. Langley and Freddie just stared at him. "As I said, what are you doing there, Chief?"

"Just taking a little water, Todd. No big deal."

"Yeah, yeah, yes it is. A big deal. You can't do that."

Langley and Freddie started to go around Philbrick to head back to their trucks, but Philbrick stepped into Langley's path.

"I said you can't do that, Chief."

"Todd."

"You're trespassing."

Langley took a step to his right, but Philbrick again blocked his way. Langley looked into Philbrick's face. "Todd," he said again.

"I can't allow you to take anything off my property," said Philbrick. "Besides, I wouldn't want you to get back in your car in your condition. That would be no good. Town hero arrested on DUI." Todd shook his head. "Not good."

"I'm not driving," said Langley.

"Oh, well, Freddie, I imagine you need another DUI like you need a hole in your head."

"We're not taking anything off your property," said Langley.

"Listen, guys," said Philbrick. "You see this frontage right here all along the river? You see that? I've got almost four hundred feet of frontage along the river here and about the same amount on my plot right across the river on the east side. So this is all mine. What's over there is mine. What's here is mine. What's in between, below and above, it's all mine. You're trespassing on my property. This water, this air, is my property."

Langley and Freddie started to move.

"Talk to my attorney," said Philbrick. "He'll tell you. I don't want anyone on my property or walking on it or dragging their little cups of water through it." He held out his hands. "Now go home, boys, and you won't have any trouble with me."

"What do you care whether we take the water or not?" said Freddie.

Todd thought for a moment. "I don't care," he finally said. "I just don't want you taking my shit."

Langley handed Philbrick the jam jar. Philbrick held the jar up to one of the streetlamps.

"Looks pretty clear to me, Chief," he said. He pushed the jar in front of Langley's face. "You see anything wrong with this?"

Langley stepped around Philbrick.

"See you around, Chief." Langley heard a plop into the water, and when he turned around he saw that Philbrick had thrown the jar into the river. "I'm sorry about Lucy Williams," Todd said, "but you're a little late, Chief, as usual."

When they walked back to their trucks, Freddie and Langley heard Todd yell out, "Be careful driving home, boys, there are cops everywhere."

Two days later Langley took a sample from the river nearer to the bridge and brought it to Dr. Schumann.

Forty-One

Wednesday, July 17, Dr. Schumann's office. "There are some usual and unusual elements in this water, Mr. Calhoun," said Dr. Schumann, "from both samples."

Langley was sitting across from Dr. Schumann.

"They are consistent with the chemicals used in the tanning industry," she said, "and with what we usually find in the water around here, iron and manganese and arsenic."

"Arsenic?" said Langley.

"There are elements of benzidene in the water and components such as 1,2-diphenylhydrazine, 3,3-dichlorobenzidine, aryl azo compounds ..."

"Whoa, whoa, Dr. Schumann."

"These are chemicals all associated with treatments for leather, things like that."

"That had to be some powerful stuff for it to still be present after all these years."

"The levels aren't very high."

"Not high enough to make people sick?"

"I don't know."

Langley paused. "Would living so close to the river or swimming in it, could that have made Lucy Williams sick?"

Dr. Schumann sighed. "It's hard to say, but this water is stressed."

Langley made a face. He didn't want to hear things like that. "What do you mean, stressed?"

"I mean in all likelihood the biology of the water is experiencing the kind of stress you and I feel when we're sick. This water is sick."

"I, um, I don't follow you."

"Mr. Calhoun, water is a living, sapient entity. It responds to outside stimuli. It can feel tranquility. It can get stressed. This water is stressed, so there's every reason to think that if you live near it, if you're exposed to it, if you live on land that is hydrated by it, it would stress you, too."

"A client of yours, a guy named Antonio Meli, gave me your book. He told me it was about the connection between your brain and water."

"Water cleanses us, Mr. Calhoun, and it has the ability to calm us down. You know that, don't you?"

"I do."

"We have these huge natural resources—oceans, lakes, streams, rivers—and we're killing them all. We are destroying these great things that not only feed us but keep us sane."

"I hadn't thought about it." Langley looked at the photos in Dr. Schumman's office. Pictures of water were everywhere. "It's depressing."

"It's scary, I'll tell you that." She looked at Langley. "What do you want to do next?"

"We should go talk to the Town Council and let them know what you found."

"I'll be happy to talk to anyone you'd like."

"Do you think the pollution might just be local?" asked Langley.

"Mr. Calhoun," she said with some finality, "there is no such thing as local pollution when it comes to water. But that isn't the point. If you have a river that cuts through

your town, and that river is sick, it's making your whole
town sick."

Forty-Two

Friday, July 19, 5:00 p.m., Langley and Delia's house. Delia was sitting in front of the TV, which is something she did rarely, and when Langley walked into the room he saw something on the TV that looked like a prehistoric, unformed fish rolling over a bumpy terrain.

When Delia saw him she pointed the remote toward the screen. The video paused, and she stood to kiss Langley. She stared into his eyes.

"Hi," she said and smiled.

"What are you watching?" All the windows in the house were open, and the soft sweet-smelling summer air floated through the room. He looked over at the windows facing the street, and he suddenly realized they had curtains. Delia had put them there, and he hadn't even noticed.

"When did you put those up?" he asked.

"Sit down," said Delia.

"What are you watching?"

"Sit," she said. "Do you want something? Can I get you a beer?" Delia never said things like that.

"What's up?"

"I want to show you something." Delia smiled. "Hold on." She pointed the clicker at the TV. "I want to start at the beginning."

Langley picked up a Tyvek video sleeve that was sitting on the table. The little blurb said it was a movie about the miracle of birth. In fact, it was called *The Miracle of Birth.*

It was for mature audiences only. There was a warning that some of the images were explicit.

The video started, and Langley looked at Delia because the video was of a couple making love on a bed. The images were graphic. The point of view would switch back and forth between the inside of the woman's vagina and the man's erect penis moving in and out of it.

Suddenly there was an explosion of white, like a rose blooming, and the billowing white cloud burst apart into thousands of sperm swimming frantically toward the camera. Langley made a face.

Soft music played on the soundtrack, and they both watched as the sperm swam through a fallopian tube toward a lone, unfertilized egg waiting for one of them.

Delia held Langley's hand. He thought the landscape of the inside of a woman's body was beautiful and delicate. It was a living, thriving garden that bloomed at the bottom of some internal sea, and he watched in silence as the sperm surrounded the egg and poked at its surface. Then one of the sperm, just as one had inside Delia's body, poked its way inside the egg, and the surface of the egg closed up because only one sperm was allowed in.

That's the one, thought Langley. That's the boy, that's the child.

Then this new fertilized egg, a tiny speck, more delicate than a drop of water, was pushed along by tiny hairs in the fallopian tube, and as it rolled and bumped along, Langley found himself feeling tense. This part made him nervous, because the entire journey seemed not only improbable but impossible. He found himself sitting there, rooting for the egg.

But then it landed in its safe harbor in the uterus. It

rolled to a stop, and the egg burst open, spilling out the very, very beginnings of life onto the uterine wall.

Langley let out a breath, and Delia shut off the TV.

"So that's what happened," said Delia, "to us, for us."

Langley smiled and tilted his head. "That wasn't you in the movie, was it?"

She laughed. He let out a sigh of relief. He knew it was a delicate time to try a joke.

"What gave me away?"

Langley shook his head and smiled.

"What are you thinking?"

"I was thinking it's amazing that anybody gets pregnant at all," Langley said.

"It's quite a trip," Delia said of the egg rolling through that tiny liquid universe. She wrapped both her arms around one of his and squeezed. "Don't be scared," she whispered.

"I am scared," and he looked at her.

"I know."

"I love you," he said, but as soon as he said it he knew it was not the right time to say something like that.

"It's gonna be great, you know."

He looked at her.

"You don't hesitate in any other part of your life, so why do you think too much when it comes to just you?" she said. Then she squeezed him and said, "No, I know why. Honey, we're going to be great."

Langley listened to the sound of Delia's voice. It was feminine, soft, soothing. There was not a trace of the harsh New Hampshire accent in it. It was full of tiny little nuances of color and expression. Her words bounced. They had inflection and warmth. Her voice didn't have that flat, toneless quality you heard from so many people today.

Delia's voice sounded like it came from another time. "You do have to call Patty and Nancy," said Delia finally.

"I know," he said. Delia looked at him.

There were two things Langley knew about Delia Reed. The first thing Langley had noticed was that even though she was busy doing something, she stopped and looked at him when he spoke. And she didn't just look at him, she saw him, watched him, her eyes were fixed on him, and Langley realized that was how she interacted with everybody and everything. She welcomed you in, and you registered with her. She didn't glance at you or avoid your gaze, she looked right at you. She was going to get as much information out of you as she could, and she wasn't afraid of you.

The other thing was how she handled things—literally handled things. Langley had a light touch. He dropped things because he never really gripped them. It was almost as though he didn't want to touch the world around him or didn't want his connection to it to be anything more than tenuous. But Delia held on to things. Her hands were strong, and when Langley saw her pick up a folder full of papers, her fingers gripped it tightly, she had control over it. He wondered what set of circumstances and genetic advantage gave her this ability to be so comfortable in the world. She felt it, she gripped it, she had control over the thing she held in her hands.

"Our baby will be strong," she said.

Forty-Three

Wednesday, July 24, 4:00 p.m., Fenton Town Hall. Maria Tull, as Chairman of the Board of Selectmen, had a small office in the Municipal Building, and she was leaning against the wall of it with her arms crossed when Langley and Dr. Schumann walked in. The look on her face clearly told them they were not welcome.

Langley introduced Dr. Schumann. Maria grunted. Langley had called Maria to try to convince her there was something in the river that made Lucy Williams sick, and something ought to be done.

"Dr. Schumann has some information ..."

"I've heard what you two are up to," Maria said. "You understand there were companies up and down and all along that river for a hundred years, dumping God knows what into it."

"Yes," said Dr. Schumann, "but the levels of some of the toxins I found ... "

"I looked you up," said Maria sharply.

"Excuse me?"

Maria went to her desk and picked up some papers. "I looked you up after Mr. Calhoun called me and said you were coming in. You have quite a rèsumè."

"Thank you."

"I didn't mean it as a compliment." Maria looked at the papers and then at Langley. "You understand that Dr. Schumann has some rather radical views."

"I wouldn't … "

Maria held up her hand, and Dr. Schumann stopped talking. Maria was a small woman, but she could command a room. "You know about this?" She handed Langley copies of some articles she had found.

"I want to talk about what is in the water," said Dr. Schumann. "Dr. Tull, the point is there is something in the water that should be recognized."

Maria handed Langley a photo. It was a picture of Dr. Schumann leading a chant to "cleanse" a lake out west on an Indian reservation, or so the caption said. She handed out more papers, like a stern teacher to underperforming pupils. There were poems Dr. Schumann had written called "Water Poems" that described the water as screaming in pain and agony. Maria had also copied reviews of Dr. Schumann's book *Betaphysics*.

"So you can see that whatever may be in the river, and I'm not saying the Oquossoc is pristine, but if there is anything in the river other than water, Dr. Schumann is going to take offense no matter what the levels. You're a radical purist, Dr. Schumann. You will object to anything, as you have. I'm not sure what credibility you have as a reasonable person."

Langley dropped the papers on Maria's desk.

"If I may just tell you what I've found," said Dr. Schumann.

"No, thank you," said Maria. "The river is clean. It's a vital part of our community, and I'm not going to allow you to come in and …" She sighed. "We've worked very hard to clean that river up, and I'm not going to allow you to spoil all that good work and get people frightened over something they have no reason to be frightened of."

"It's not just that the water will make people physically sick, Dr. Tull. Pollution makes people mentally unfit, as well, " said Dr. Schumann.

"Maria, Lucy Williams thought she was getting sick from the river," said Langley.

"And I feel bad about that," she said to Langley, "but one person dying of cancer is not going to prove anything, nor is it going to prompt me to spend town resources looking into it, getting everybody worked up and concerned. You may want a heap of legal trouble, Mr. Calhoun. You seem to live in a state of chaos. I don't. Certainly I don't want to do so for no good reason." She paused. "Do you enjoy upsetting people in this town? Hurting your friends?"

"My friends?" said Langley.

Maria picked up a copy of Dr. Schumann's book and opened it where she had a bookmark. Langley noticed that it was an endearingly feminine bookmark, pink with small delicate flowers and some sort of saying or quote written in delicate script. She read aloud, "You may think, when you see trees, manicured lawns and cultivated gardens, that you are surrounded by nature, but you are not." She closed the book with a flourish and chuckled in a sarcastic way.

"Now, I may not have a Ph.D. from Harvard, Dr. Schumann, but when I see a tree, I think I see nature. I'm pretty sure I'm right about that."

"You're an angry person," Dr. Schumann said.

"Dr. Schumann, please. Maria, you can't just discount what she's found," said Langley.

"Mr. Calhoun here must be worried about his fading celebrity, so …"

Dr. Schumann made a sound of disgust. "Let's go," she said. "This is insulting."

"We're going to get that bridge built," Maria said suddenly. "We're going to develop that part of town."

Langley looked at her. He had no idea why she'd said that. He looked at Dr. Schumann. Then he looked back at Maria, but he didn't say anything. He wanted to make sure he had heard what Maria said correctly.

"Lucy Williams doesn't benefit from your crusade." Maria made a face. "You should take your past problems, Mr. Calhoun, and learn to channel them into something more productive."

This was exactly why Langley didn't like to stick his neck out any more. Someone, somewhere, was always going to try to accuse him of trying to avenge Danny's death or to overcompensate for the failings of his own family, say he had an ax to grind, and he was motivated by something other than trying to do the right thing. Langley himself was wary of self-righteous people, because more often than not they did have something to hide. They did have an ax to grind or a skeleton in the closet. That's why most good people stay out of the fray, because they know if they take a stand, something about their past will be used to discredit them.

Maria pushed herself off the wall and took a step toward her two guests. "Oh, I wanted to say, Mr. Calhoun, that I saw Danny and Emily the other day. They had an appointment." Danny and Emily were Brian's kids, Langley's nephew and niece, and they were patients at Maria's dental practice.

Maria's voice had changed. It was warm and kind, and Langley looked up and smiled. He knew she had changed the subject, but she seemed to want to say something nice. "They seemed quite devastated, poor things."

Langley and Dr. Schumann walked down the stairs and into the Selectmen's Chambers. He stopped for a moment, and Dr. Schumann stayed off to the side. Langley was fuming. He was angry at the pettiness, the shortsightedness.

"Goddamnit," he said.

"Forget it," said Dr. Schumann.

Forty-Four

Thursday, August 1, 8:00 p.m., Langley and Delia's house.
The bridge to nowhere was making progress. The old
wooden bridge still sat in the field, spanning a patch of dry
land. A local photographer started selling postcards with a
photo of the new bridge on it with the headline, "Welcome
to Fenton, NH! Gateway to ... Fenton, NH!" The same guy
had another one showing people posing on the old bridge,
on dry land, as though they were fishing off it, their lines
plopped on the dirt, and the headline said, "Gone fishin' in
Fenton, NH."

Langley put Dr. Schumann's book on a table in the
living room. He picked it up at least once a day. He was
intrigued by it. He was moving away from the idea that it
was silly or farfetched. The image of the tiny egg floating
down that river of fluids, that quiet yet determined journey
Delia had shown him, had made him think about the
Oquossoc as something other than just a river flowing
through town. He picked up the book once again and
started to read the jacket.

*A magnificent aqua-planet was pushed by galactic
winds through the universe and washed over the desert
earth, the young uninhabited earth, just as a wave washes
over a rock on the shore, and it bathed the bald planet with
billions of living things — all the living things now on the
Earth.*

It was an odd image, a bubble of water traveling

through the universe with species suspended inside it, waiting to be released.

Dr. Schumann believed water was living. She believed water reacted to its surroundings just as we react to water. Langley was particularly struck by a passage she wrote about how boat engines had the same effect on water as a knife does on skin. She advocated days of prayer in which the whole world participated to start healing the waters of the earth.

Langley didn't think her argument was really that crazy. Life was not possible without water, she argued, so why did we think water was not living? Places without water were dead zones, deserts, and she mentioned the lifeless, waterless planets floating around us in the universe. She wrote that the water in oceans, seas, lakes and rivers and streams was no different than the blood flowing through our veins. That was why, she wrote, we react so strongly to water itself, why we are drawn to it during times of stress and anxiety, because returning to the water is like returning to your primordial being, to a time when you were new and clean and healthy.

And, she argued, what happens when those bodies of water become anxious and stressed themselves? As our water has become dirtier, the planet has become correspondingly more confused and angry. "There are fewer places to turn to for solace," she wrote.

Langley couldn't argue with that. He thought of his little child growing inside Delia. He thought of that tiny unfertilized egg rolling to its destiny.

Langley put the book down and went around the house, looking for his map of New Hampshire. He found it in the bottom drawer of one of the kitchen cabinets and spread it out on the dining room table.

He looked at it and shook his head. It was no trick to notice that the rivers and streams creeping through the land looked like veins. Everybody noticed that. It was nothing new. But he stood over the map, staring at it. For the first time he looked at the water on the map and not the land, not the towns or the roads or the mountains. He looked at the blue, Lake Winnipesaukee and the crowded group of lakes known as the Lakes Region. And he looked at the Piscataqua River, the mighty but short river with the powerful current.

Langley had never thought of the Oquossoc as anything more than the relatively small stretch of water that cut through Fenton. He never thought about where it started, how long it was, and what other towns it went through. The river was a little more than forty-seven miles long, traveled southeastward and cut through the towns of Farmington, Rochester, Fenton and Dover before emptying into the Piscataqua.

He looked at all the spidery tributaries and back channels and streams and brooks. Water had inched its way everywhere into the land. There was water literally everywhere you looked, and it all led to the huge bowl of the Atlantic Ocean. All those rivers and bodies of water pouring, pouring, pouring into the Atlantic, carrying everything with it.

Langley wondered why he'd never thought of the water the way he did his own blood, as Dr. Schumann said. You never think of your blood as a separate part of your body, he thought, but your blood is an essential part of your muscles, your brain, your cells.

But we think of water and land as separate, as two

separate things. Langley looked at the water threading through the land. If the water dried up, the land would die, just as your muscles and eyesight and life itself would fade away as soon as your blood stopped flowing. Why did we not think of water as a living thing?

Langley smiled at his own thoughts. He laughed silently to himself. Dr. Schumann would be happy with him.

Maybe water was the biggest, most obvious life form on the planet, only we didn't even know it. Why wouldn't it feel? Why wouldn't it have memory? But because we haven't thought of water as a living, sentient being covering two thirds of the earth, it's easier to trash it, poison it, dump on it, kill it. Why would we think something that covers two-thirds of the earth, that is two-thirds of your own body, something that comes pouring out of trees when you cut them down, that drips out of grape vines, that clings to the grass in the morning ... what would lead us to believe this is not, in fact, a living thing?

Langley thought of all the things the water carried with it, its injuries and junk, and wondered if the ocean had an unlimited capacity to continue to receive all that injury.

All we are is rain, Lucy Williams had said. Goddamnit, Langley thought, *goddamnit*. Maybe she was right.

Maybe Lucy was right.

He didn't think either of them was so crazy, after all. Not at all.

Forty-Five

Monday, August 5, 3:00 a.m., Langley and Delia's house.
Langley's phone rang. The sound of an electrical bell
ringing seemed to fill the entire house with some sense of
foreboding. Langley and Delia sat up in bed. Langley had
been awake anyway. He went into the living room because
he no longer kept the phone on his nightstand like he did
when he was a cop. He picked it up off the table and looked
at who was calling. It was his father.

"Dad?" But he heard Vance speak.

"Hi, Langley. I'm sorry to call at this time, but I didn't
…"

"Is everything OK?"

"Your father had a nightmare. He had a dream about
Danny. He can't seem to shake it, and he's sitting on the bed
crying."

"Oh, Jesus," said Langley.

"I'm sorry," said Vance.

"Don't be sorry. Do you think I should come over?"

"He's been up for more than an hour, and he keeps
shaking his head, and he can't stop crying."

"I'll be right there."

"Thank you, honey," said Vance with genuine feeling.

Delia had come into the living room. "My father had a
dream about Danny. Something hit him pretty hard."

"Do you want me to come with you?"

"No, no, I'm not going to be long."

"You're going to be up all night."
"You don't mind coming?"
"I'll keep Vance company."

Forty-Six

Monday, August 5, 4:15 a.m., Tim Calhoun's house.
Langley went into his father's bedroom, and he saw his old
man sitting on the edge of his bed, clutching a towel,
hunched over, crying, looking as old as he had ever seen
him.

Langley sat down and put his arm around his father,
who looked up and started to cry even more when he saw
his son.

Danny, Langley's older brother and the twin of his
brother Brian, had been dead for more than thirty years, but
the pain is constant and never very far away. It doesn't ever
take much to scratch that pain and have it bleed out all over
the place, and that is what Langley figured had happened in
his father's dream.

"Danny was at the beach, he was lying in the water at
the beach, and the waves were coming right over him, and I
was trying to pull him out of the water, and he had his eyes
open, but I knew he was dead," said his father. "I had this
feeling that if I could get him out of the water, he would
stay alive, and I was trying to tell your mother that Danny
was going to be all right, that he was fine."

Langley's mother, Tim Calhoun's beloved wife
Maureen, had been dead for almost ten years.

"But when I pulled him out of the water and up onto the
sand, I knew he was dead, and your mother said to me,
'Danny's dead, and he's never coming back.' He was blue

and cold, and it looked like he had been in the water forever."

Langley could only shake his head. It sounded brutal. He didn't say anything, just kept rubbing his father's back.

"What your mother said really scared me."

"Why?"

"Because I thought she meant he was never going to come back in my dreams. The only place I can ever see your brother is in my dreams. He's alive and laughing most of the time in my dreams, and what if he doesn't come back? What if I never see him again?"

Langley had also dreamed about Danny. The dreams were mostly violent and terror filled, and they used to make Langley wake up screaming. Langley had been climbing the same tree as Danny, and Danny had been on the branch above him. Langley was the one who had playfully yanked on Danny's arm and sent him crashing down into another limb that had split a gash up the entire length of Danny's torso.

Langley had jumped down off his low branch, looked at his brother, run into the house and pulled on his father's arm to get him to come running out to see his brother. That was when he'd heard his father scream, and Langley could never bear the sound of a man screaming. It frightened him.

"Danny isn't going to stop visiting you, Pop," Langley said now.

"I don't think I could take it if he did. I can't go on and not see him. I wait and wait and wait for him to come. I never think it's a dream."

"Don't worry, Dad, he'll come around again."

"Do you ever dream about him?"

"Of course I do," said Langley, but he didn't say anything more.

"That's good."

"And mom, too," but Langley had never had a dream about his mother. Not once.

"Brian must, too, then, right?"

"I'm sure he does," said Langley. "I'm sure he does."

"That's good," said Tim Calhoun. "That's good." His tears were drying now, and the convulsive breathing had slowed. The old man wiped his face. "I'm okay," he said, but he was far from okay.

Langley smiled at his father, at his willful defiance ever to seem weak or scared. But Langley also realized that was ending, too. His father was seventy years old. The young army soldier was now an old soldier, no longer boasting that he had the same size waist he'd had during basic training and could still wear his old uniform if he wanted to. Yes, the young man in uniform, the one with his arm around his comrades in Saigon, grinning, with a cigarette dangling out of his mouth and a can of Black Label in his one free hand, was now an old man, sitting in the dark, trembling because of a dream about the son he'd lost a long time ago.

Langley grimaced. Life is hard, he thought to himself, and his eyes filled with tears. He wanted his father to be happy and free of the burden of grief, but that wasn't going to happen. Old Irishmen are sentimental.

"Do you want any tea or anything?"

"Yeah, yes, some tea would be nice." The old man didn't even joke that what he really needed was a drink. It would have been his standard, stock joke, but he didn't even say that. Langley was relieved to see some of this fire go away, but he also realized that his father's once legendary energy, the energy that had allowed him to drink Wild Turkey at eight in the morning and still go out hunting for forty-eight hours straight, was failing him a little bit. The old man, bit by bit by bit, was giving out.

He lifted his father up, and they walked into the living room. Vance and Delia were sitting on the couch, each with a cup of coffee.

"Mr. Calhoun would like a little spot of tea," said Langley with half a smile on his face.

Without saying anything, Vance rose and went into the kitchen. She loved the old man, too.

Delia stood and took Tim Calhoun by the elbow and sat him down next to her. She knew what to do. She placed the old man's hand on her belly, and he leaned over and put his ear against her so he could hear his grandchild swimming in the dark.

Forty-Seven

Saturday, August 31, 10:00 a.m., Langley and Delia's house. Langley was sitting in the chair in the living room, his cell phone in his hand. He needed to call his ex-wife Julia and let her know that he and Delia were pregnant.

He was nervous and proud at the same time but was unsure of how his two daughters would react. As little as he actually knew them, he felt they would be excited and happy to have a new sibling. When he told that to Delia, she looked at him and made a face that said *you might be crazy, honey.* So he sat in the chair, just staring at the phone.

Delia came into the room, holding a cup of tea. She was in the full bloom of her pregnancy. She looked extremely beautiful, extremely healthy. Her face was maybe the most beautiful human landscape Langley had ever seen. He was happy she was there in the room with him, so he dialed the phone.

When Julia answered, Langley's voice was low and steady, and he told his ex-wife that he and Delia were having a baby. There was a little bit of silence. Julia and her second husband, who lived in Pennsylvania, were not able to have children of their own.

"When?" said Julia, and she cleared her throat.

He didn't want to answer that. "She's due at the end of the year."

There was another bit of silence.

"Really?"

"You have to understand that Delia has been asking me to call you for a while."

More silence.

"I don't doubt that," said Julia. "Do you know if it's a boy or girl?"

"Well," said Langley, "the thing of it is," and he told her the story about how the baby was a Down Syndrome child, and there was an uncertain road ahead.

"Well ...God," said Julia. She let out a long sigh and seemed to be on the verge of tears. "Good for you for having the baby." Her voice was shaky.

"I'm sorry I didn't call for so long," he said. He was amazed at how much of his old self returned when he was talking to Julia. It was almost as though a switch was turned on. He became his old, fumbling self.

"I have to, um, go," said Julia.

"Wait a second." Langley asked if he could speak to the girls, but they were not at home. Julia asked if Langley could call back and tell them the news himself. He said he would.

"Julia," he said just before they hung up. "I want to, um, be more, ah, in touch without being disruptive. With the kids, I mean."

"How do you propose to do that?" Julia asked with just a little edge in her voice.

"I don't mean I'm all of a sudden going to be their father ..."

"Langley," she said, her voice full of impatience, "just by saying those words shows how far you have to go with this. You *are* their father."

"I know, I know, but they're doing well, right?"

She sighed. "Ask them for yourself."

"But is everything okay?"

"Langley, if one of our kids was in serious trouble I would tell you."

"I know you would. I know. I can ease into this thing, and I know they're not children any more. I've missed a lot, but I have this ... goal, if I can tell you."

"Of course you can." Her voice was clear again.

"I just want to work at it so that when the time comes around for Patty to graduate from college and get married, I can be there, and I want to have her happy I'm there."

"Then just don't fade away anymore. College is not as far away as you think," said Julia. "And call when something is happening that affects us all. I'm not at all sure the girls are going to be happy, you know."

"I know, I know."

"Ease into it."

"Okay."

"Don't try to Facebook them. They won't want you to know what's going on there."

He laughed. "Facebook. That's not going to happen."

"Okay. Well, you've never even promised this before, so I actually think it's a start."

"I'll call the kids later on."

"Call after seven or so. I'll make sure both are home." She paused. "Just be forewarned, I have no idea how they'll react. I have to say I'm a little stunned myself."

"Even if they're mad and they talk to me," Langley said about the girls, "it's a start."

Julia sighed. "Brian gets home soon, huh?"

"Yeah."

"Good luck with that." Julia had never liked Brian, but she had written her ex-father-in-law, saying how much it anguished her that he was in jail and how much it scared Patty and Nancy. The children had known Brian as a good man, as a kind uncle, and so to see him put in jail for reasons they could not fathom, reasons their own father had to do with, scared them. These were emotions too complicated and unpleasant to try to untangle as a teen and a pre-teen.

"We'll deal with it when he gets out, I guess."

"Oh, good," said Julia with complete and practiced bitterness. "That's the Calhoun way."

"He'll get out, and we'll welcome him if he wants us to."

"You'll do what you're going to do, you and your father." Then she said, "Langley?"

"Yes."

"Call your children."

Forty-Eight

Later that same morning. Langley talked to Patty and Nancy. He told them about the pregnancy and how the baby boy might have something wrong with him, but he and Delia were going to love the baby and give it a happy life. He did not say to the girls that the child was their sibling or that they had any obligation to know or even acknowledge the new child. He just said he and Delia were having a child together, and it was a happy thing.

"I'm going to try to keep more in touch, okay?" He was talking to his older daughter Patty, who was thirteen.

"Okay."

"Can I ask you how you feel about the baby?"

"I think if you're having the baby and it might be sick, that's pretty cool of you to do," she said.

Langley wanted to tell her he loved her, too, but he knew that would turn her off, so he didn't. "I'll call you soon."

"Okay."

"If you want to call me, too, you can."

"I know." She sounded sullen, but Langley thought she didn't sound too sullen.

"I'll call you to tell you what's going on, okay?"

"Okay."

His conversation with Nancy was less successful. He asked if he could call her, and she said Patty would let her know what was going on.

"You can call me if you want," he said.

She made a noise.

"Just do me a favor, if you can. A small one," Langley said.

"What?" she asked very quietly.

"I'm going to call, and I'm going to ask for you, and all I want you to do is come to the phone. You don't have to speak, but I want you to listen, even just for a little bit. I won't take up too much time."

"Fine," she said. Her voice was a little timid whisper.

"Okay," said Langley. "I'll talk to you soon." He didn't call either of them honey or anything else cute or endearing, because he knew he would sound stupid.

He called the next week, and Patty took his call, but Nancy didn't, and that's the way it went.

Forty-Nine

Thursday, September 12, 6:30 .a.m., Langley and Delia's house. Someone sent Langley a package in the mail. His name and address were printed on a small white label. There was no return address. He opened it up and saw a copy of the contract the town had signed with Todd Philbrick

The first thing he noticed was that there did not seem to be any money involved. Philbrick "bought" the thirty acres on the west side of the river from his own father, and the transaction involved a series of incentives, including paying his father when a certain percentage of the land had been developed. It was a complicated contract, and Langley marked the passages he wanted another opinion on. If the property was not developed by the end of the calendar year, this year, the town would have the option of buying the land, also at no cost but with fees attached.

Langley made a note in the margin: "Will the building of the bridge be considered development?" He wondered if Philbrick would make the legal argument that since he built the bridge, he had developed the property and therefore did not lose the rights to it.

Philbrick was responsible for the property taxes while he owned it, but Langley thought the lot seemed to have an extremely low appraisal for a piece of property that was located along the water. Then he came across a section that was a complete surprise. It was about something called air rights. Langley sat up in his chair.

As he read it through and made notes, he got the impression that even if Todd Philbrick lost the deed to the land itself, he would still own the air above it, which essentially meant he controlled the development of the property no matter who owned the land.

Langley read the section a couple of times and then dialed Ed Lustig. He told him what he had just read.

Ed chuckled. "Air rights. I know what they are."

"Am I reading that right?"

"Yeah, the guy owns the air. He owns it."

"How can you own the air?"

"It's a legal concept. It's legit."

"How can it be legit?"

"It's a perfectly legal concept."

Langley remembered the night he and Freddie had been trying to take a sample of the water, and Todd had said something about how everything in and above the river was his. Langley hadn't understood the comment then, but he did now. "How does a contract like this even get approved?'

"You're talking about a small New England town. You know how these things work. This is a surprise to you?"

"Is there any way to stop it?"

"I haven't seen the contract, but I doubt it. You could just let it go."

"Do you think the town could argue that the bridge is actually a development, and he might not even lose the lease?"

"You can argue anything," said Lustig, "but even as far as that goes it's not a bad argument legally speaking. I've seen a lot flimsier arguments prevail."

"Is that something you can do?"
"You mean take up the case?"
"Yeah."
"No, no, not me, buddy boy."
"Do you know anybody who would?"
"Your own lawyer. You like her, don't you?"
Chloe Webb. "She's great," said Langley.
"She's not afraid of the town."
"Not at all. Not afraid of anybody."
"Have her read the contract."

Fifty-One

Monday, September 23, 6:30 p.m., Langley and Delia's living room. Chloe Brooke had a tattoo of a snake—at least, Langley thought it was a snake—crawling up behind her collar bone and over her shoulder.

The head of the reptile was resting on her left breast. It was all Langley could do to keep his eyes settled in the right place as Chloe leaned over the contract she had laid out on the living room table. She was wearing a Red Sox sweatshirt inside out, as though she had just come from the gym, and she had made a cut on the collar that opened it up even more.

Langley took a quick look at Delia, who was sitting curled up in one of the big chairs, and her half-amused expression told him the jig was up. He adjusted his posture and made sure his eyes stayed where they ought to be.

Chloe kept turning the pages of the contract. When she got to the last page, she flipped the stapled document over, picked up her glass of wine and drank.

"The idea of air rights comes from Roman law," she said, "which basically said that whoever owns the land owns it down to hell and up to heaven." She sighed. "That makes Mr. Philbrick quite a land baron."

"How does that happen?"

"Lawyers," said Chloe.

Langley sighed.

Chloe stood and stretched. She went and stood at the

window and looked out at the street, then turned around and faced Langley and Delia. "I'm tired," she said.

"We can pick it up again sometime this week," said Langley.

"No, I'm tired," she said. "I, um ..." But she didn't finish her sentence and she sat back down on the couch. Langley looked over at Delia, who made a face as if to say she didn't know what Chloe was thinking.

Chloe took another look at the contract and then pushed it away. She rubbed her face with her hands. "I'm not afraid of a fight," she said.

"I know that."

"But lately I've been thinking how much I can do."

The reason Langley had hired Chloe more than ten years ago was because she was a fighter. She defended underdogs, destitute rape victims, kids who had been arrested for a bag of pot in their backpacks. She didn't particularly like cops, and she had once said her goal was to fight against every dumb law that every politician had ever passed.

She took on the cases of people who had been swindled out of their money and robbed of their identity. She went after cops and firefighters and anyone else she thought had done something wrong and hidden behind their unions or their badges or their uniforms. She didn't shy away from anything.

If she disliked cops, she liked politicians even less, but she happened to like Langley.

"I don't know how much more I want to do," she said a little sadly.

Langley looked over at Delia.

"It never stops," said Chloe. "My office phone doesn't

stop ringing."

She looked up, and Langley saw that she did look tired. He wasn't going to ask her not to help. If she didn't want to, that was her business, but he wasn't going to talk her out of it. There was a moment of quiet in the room.

"Listen, the contract is solid, there's no question of that," Chloe said. "Your best bet is to find out how it was passed, if it was subject to the proper public hearing and if it adheres to the town's no-bid guidelines. If it's all up to speed, the only thing that might be in your favor is to expose it, get the press to write about it and see if the public reacts."

"Okay," said Langley.

"But you have to rely on people doing the right thing." Chloe sighed. She picked up the contract again. "The land rights expire on the thirty-first of December, and the air rights he owns forever."

"Is that unusual?" said Langley.

"Air rights are a normal abnormality," said Chloe, "but owning the air rights in perpetuity is not usual." She looked down at the papers again. "This contract is pretty favorable to the contractor, and I say that with some sense of understatement."

Langley nodded his head. "Sorry I couldn't do more." She picked up her purse. "What are you going to do?"

"I don't know," Langley said.

"Look. This is not about the contract, but it's just my opinion. It seems to me that you have twenty-five or thirty acres of riverfront property, usually some of the most coveted land anywhere, and it's gone unsold for decades. What does that tell you?"

"The story has always been that everybody thinks no

one will come to Fenton, no matter what you build. I mean, we're close to the outlet malls in Kittery, that kind of thing." He frowned. "I think everybody simply thinks it's a case of town dysfunction."

"Can it be that dysfunctional?"

"It takes forever to get anything done here, believe me."

"They got rid of you pretty quick." Chloe smiled.

That was true. When Langley's chief of police contract had been up a few years ago, it took one meeting for the town not to renew it. He had been chief for eight years. That was how he'd gotten into the private investigation business with Ed Lustig.

"You told me the town manager — what's her name?"

"Maria Tull."

"You told me that when you went to see her about the quality of the water, she said no matter what you were trying to do, they were going to develop that land anyway, right?"

"Right," said Langley, who then looked up. "You're thinking something is actually wrong with the river."

"And as a consequence there's something wrong with the land that's right next to it."

"Jesus."

"Whatever is going on over there with the bridge and them protecting that little building has something to do with that," Chloe said.

Langley nodded. He could see the logic of that.

"Listen, I want you to talk to a friend of mine," Chloe said. She reached into her bag and took out a pen and piece of paper.

"Anybody you think might help."

"He's a real estate agent. His family has been buying

and selling property in New Hampshire for a long time. He might know something." She leaned over, kissed Langley on the cheek and handed him the slip of paper on which she had written a name and number. "I've got to go. I've got to pick up some pumpkins."

Fifty-One

Friday, September 27, noon, Chief Darrow's office.
"Listen, I'm sorry this has taken so long." Chief Darrow
was behind his desk, and he pointed to a box on the floor.

"You don't have to apologize to me, Chief."

"No, I made a promise, but we're short-staffed, and …"

"You need an extra cop?"

Darrow looked at Langley and smiled. "I could use an
extra cop. I could use you, but we're on a hiring freeze."

Langley waved the comment off and sat down. "I'm
retired."

"What I'm going to tell you is going to make you
unhappy."

"Okay."

"It turns out Lucy Williams had a paramour."

"That surprises me, but it doesn't make me unhappy."

"Todd Philbrick. These here," Darrow nodded in the
direction of the box, "are transcripts of emails back and
forth between Lucy and your friend Todd."

Langley leaned over and took the cover off the box and
looked inside. "This is recent?"

"Well, not so long ago. It stopped some time ago."

"I'm still not sure why I should be mad."

"Although nothing is spelled out, and this goes back a
few years now, it looks as though she was asking Todd for
advice on how to sell her house, and he kept telling her he

was interested in buying it because he needed more property along the river."

"Okay."

"I can't say it was legit or not …"

"What was legit, his love or his offer?"

"Either."

"That fucking guy," said Langley

"Whatever happened, the affair seems to have broken off about a year ago, a little more, and of course real estate had bottomed out before that, and nothing ever happened."

"Anything you can get him on?"

"No."

"Asshole."

"No doubt, but not a criminal."

"Not yet," said Langley.

Fifty-Two

Saturday, October 5, 5:30 p.m., Fenton, NH. Langley had never met anyone before who looked like a computer chip, but this kid was it.

Everything about him was thin and angular and cool. His face was planed into perfection. His shirt, his sports jacket, the crease in his pants, the points in the collar of his shirt, the glint in his eyes, all of them were paper thin. He was smoothed out to the point of being inhuman. His legs were crossed, and they seemed almost to melt into each other. His eyes were cobalt blue. They looked like two digital beads, slightly dead like badly realized computer animated eyes.

They were sitting outside on the sidewalk at a small coffeeshop called The Morning Buzzz. It was a cool day. Leaves were swirling around their feet.

"I looked at that land," Ted Perkins said about the property in the Shoals near Lucy Williams' house.

Langley had handed him a copy of Todd Philbrick's contract, but the young man took no notice of it. He didn't even pick it up, as though he didn't want to put his fingerprints on it.

"And?" Langley asked.

"The kid who owns it wants to sell the land, but he wants to hold onto the air rights. It isn't a good deal for anyone who wants to develop it, not the way it's set up now."

"Is that the only thing holding it up?"

"There's something about it that's not right. When I talked to Philbrick he mentioned he might be able to increase the lot size. I thought he might have some deals with the adjoining property owners. There's a house next to the lot you could probably get for a song that would add another half acre, which would be good for parking."

Lucy Williams' house. Some of the emails Langley had read from Todd Philbrick to Lucy talked about her house. Todd had asked Lucy to talk to him first if she was thinking about selling it. He'd hinted that selling it would relieve some of her stress and could possibly help with her tight money situation. Maybe the reference was to the Marabellas. Their house had been filled with packing boxes the day Langley visited.

"You'd think someone would want that land," Langley said.

"Land is not so precious just yet that people are willing to get tied up with Philbrick. Everyone I talked to came away with a bad feeling about the guy. They just knew it was not going to be worth the aggravation." He looked down for a second. "My feeling is that at some point the town of Fenton will run out of developable property, and just by being the only lot left, it will be valuable to somebody. Those air rights will be worth something someday, believe me."

"What if the property is polluted?"

The kid pulled at the cuffs of his shirt. He looked off into the distance. He didn't say anything and then turned the corners of his mouth down and shook his head.

"I met a woman, who has since died, who lived in that house you're talking about. She said the water in the

Oquossoc made her sick. She lives right next to that land." Langley deliberately used the present tense. "She died convinced that her illness, and others in her family and her neighborhood, were because of the poisons over there. Could that be the real reason no one's bought it?"

"That's the town's business, or the state's, or the feds. I don't know." He took a deep, bored breath.

Perkins shrugged his shoulders.

"Just for the sake of argument, what if I were to ask you what you knew under oath?"

The young man sighed. "I"m doing you a favor. Actually, I'm doing Chloe a favor. So, you know, I mean, that is not going to happen."

"Well, thanks for your time. I appreciate it."

"Is that it?" The kid wasn't annoyed. He just wanted to make sure they were done.

"Yes, thank you." Langley held out his hand, and Perkins shook it even as he was turning to leave. "Chloe said you were from New Hampshire," Langley said.

"That's right." Perkins' voice had an annoyed, singsong tone in it now.

"Where are you from?" Langley asked.

"Gilmanton."

"Gilmanton?"

"Gilmanton Iron Works, if you need to know. Why?" Perkins looked up. "What is this? Some sort of tribal thing? You and I are brothers in arms?"

"No," said Langley sadly, "I'm just curious."

"I went to Dartmouth." Then he looked at Langley. "UNH?"

Langley watched as the foreign object before him disappeared.

Fifty-Three

Monday, October 5, 4:30 p.m., Fenton, NH. Langley walked along the path that edged the big bend in the Oquossoc near the new bridge site. There were kids in the nearby park, throwing a Frisbee, and some dogwalkers carrying their small bags of dog shit.

He heard the sound of a seagull crying overhead. It was dusk. The bird had its wings outstretched, and it was floating along on the cool breeze. It was all by itself, but it was calling out to someone, and it flew off into the distance. Langley watched it fly into the sun. When his eyes lowered they settled on an orange traffic cone sticking out of the Oquossoc. It was low tide, and the water was trickling by.

He looked at all the rusted junk in the riverbed, and it disgusted him. He thought of the water just rolling in and out over that crap day after day, year after year, just mixing into the water. The surface of the river was covered with autumn leaves. He wondered if the water felt the memories of all the junk and hurt that it carried out to the ocean.

He was carrying an envelope full of some of the emails Darrow had printed out for him. He was looking for Todd Philbrick, and he was going to ask him about his relationship with Lucy and what he might know about any pollution on the land.

It was cold, and he wanted to get back home. He was thinking about what Schumann had said, that water was a living, conscious thing.

Langley looked down at the slow moving water of the river. It ran low below the stones and granite shards. The old stones had dried brown in the sun, and the riverbed looked ancient, prehistoric. The seagull was now floating in the water all by itself.

There was a small patch of oil or gas swirling on the surface of the river. He looked at it briefly, thinking it was nothing more than diesel from a boat that had cruised somewhere far up the river, but now he didn't really know where it might have come from. He looked at the dirty traffic cone again.

A river is not technically a river if it is tidal. The old timers around Fenton reminded people that even the Piscataqua River was not technically a river. It was what long ago they'd called a drowned valley, and that seemed fitting enough even for the mild Oquossoc. A drowned valley. Sometimes you could see the water flowing inland, filling up the old valley as it had done for eons.

The bridge crew seemed to be working just as they always had. Then he saw a big guy walking over in his direction with a heavy wrench in his hand.

"Can I help you?" the man said.

"Todd around?"

"This is private property."

"Okay," said Langley. "No, it's not, but okay."

"You a reporter?"

"I'm the former chief of police."

"You're the guy," the man said.

"I'm the guy, yes."

"Todd's not around."

"Just tell him to get in touch with me soon. I have something to give him, some emails between him and Lucy Williams," said Langley.

"Anything else?"

"Yeah. You should be careful when you walk up to someone with a wrench like that," said Langley. "This is New Hampshire. People have guns."

Fifty-Four

Tuesday, October 8, 11:45 a.m., Fenton, NH. "I don't know how I missed this." Britney Suwako was looking at the contract Langley had just given her. It was Chloe's copy, the one that was all marked up, and there were a few Post-It notes added by Langley. She kept flipping through the pages. "Wow," she said. "Wow, wow, wow.

Dr. Schumann then handed her a printed out report of the chemicals she had found in the water.

"Lucy Williams was keeping samples. She was telling everyone the water was making her sick," Langley said.

"I want to be very clear," said Dr. Schumann. "I don't know the source of these chemicals."

"It could be anywhere, you mean?"

Dr. Schumann nodded her head.

"Up river?"

"Up in Canada, for all I know," Dr. Schumann said. "We don't know."

"Got it," said Britney. "We've got the air rights thing down, that's solid, but that's a different story than the pollutants." Britney put the contract down and squeezed the bridge between her eyes. "That could get us into trouble."

"You don't have to mention Lucy Williams. Just report what's in the water. That will get people's attention."

"Philbrick's lawyers. Private attorneys for the people living next door. *Litigators.*"

"There are these emails." He handed Britney a folder.

"What are these again?"

"Emails between Lucy and Todd Philbrick."

"About what?"

"Philbrick was stringing her along. I think he was trying to get her to sell her house so he could expand his lot size. I think he was trying to scam her out of it."

"Does he say that in these emails?"

"No."

She handed him back the folder with a look that said she wasn't interested. "How can I go with the pollutants if I can't prove anything?" Britney said.

"Just tell people what I found in the samples," said Dr. Schumann.

"You just said you don't know the source of what's in the water. You said you don't know where it comes from. You said … Listen. The sad thing is that Lucy Williams should have sued when she was alive. She could have forced the town to take water and soil samples from her well, from the well next door, but that didn't happen."

She looked at the two people sitting in front of her. "Where can I get independent testing done for the new samples coming out of the river? If I can get those, and they still report the shit that you're saying is in the river, then I'll go with that. Nothing about Lucy Williams, but I will go with those results," Britney said.

Fifty-Five

Sunday, October 27, 7:00 a.m., Langley and Delia's house.
The *Fenton Herald* had a story on the front page of the
paper: "Who owns the air (and the water underneath)?"
There were pictures of how the Oquossoc looked today and
what it had looked like one hundred years ago. There was
the entire text of the contract and the usual quotes from
town officials—Maria Tull and Town Attorney Eb Webb—
claiming the contract was legal and above board.

The newspaper printed an old picture of Dr. Schumann
sitting cross-legged on the banks of the Rio Grande,
reciting a poem. Langley was unhappy with the way Dr.
Schumann was portrayed. She came across as a bit of a
lunatic, as someone who may or may not have ties with
some of the radical, violent environmental groups.

She was perhaps the sexiest part of the story, the most
colorful, and people ended up talking as much about her as
they did about Todd Philbrick.

Soon there were satellite trucks parked alongside the
river, and reporters could be found in the coffee shops and
pizza parlors, asking any local they could find if they had
any opinion on air rights.

Unlike Langley, Dr. Schumann was not afraid to get in
front of the camera or to talk to *The New York Times*,
because she was determined to get her message out. She
was also the only one who was not afraid to bring up the
name Lucy Williams. She held a picture of Lucy in front of

the cameras and said this woman had died because of the pollution in the Oquossoc.

She was careful. She didn't name any names, didn't blame anyone, didn't say anything too specific. When asked if she could prove it, she said, "Lucy Williams is dead, isn't she?"

"Maybe she talks too much," Delia said when they were watching the news one night.

Langley looked at Delia. "Maybe," he said. "Maybe she doesn't know what else to do."

The article in the paper also reported that Todd Philbrick did not respond to repeated phone calls. He could also be seen slamming his car door in the faces of various TV news reporters.

"The guy who never shuts up finally stops talking," said Freddie Ouellette.

There was also an editorial calling for a special town meeting on the matter.

Langley's phone started to ring immediately. His father called him to say that people were also calling him, old friends from town asking him what the hell his son was doing, asking why he was trying to ruin the town. Tim Calhoun told even his oldest friends that his son was his own man, and if they had a problem with Langley they could call him directly.

Ed Lustig called to ask him how he was holding up.

Delia sat on her yoga rug in the living room with her legs crossed, palms up and eyes closed.

Fifty-Six

Wednesday, November 20, Tim Calhoun's house. It was 4:00 a.m., and Vance and Tim Calhoun and Delia and Langley stood in the dark kitchen of Tim's kitchen. It was dark and cold, and it reminded Langley of the time, years and years ago, Langley and Brian and Danny had risen early in the morning to go cut a Christmas tree down in the middle of the town woods.

It had been a little adventure, a great adventure as Langley remembered it, but he didn't often think of it because Danny had died the next summer. That had been the last Christmas they were all together, but Langley was remembering the moment they'd all gathered in the kitchen and drunk coffee and gone out to cut the tree.

Langley and Delia were at the house now to see Tim and Vance off on the trip to pick up Brian. Brian had initially tried to insist on flying home, but the old man would have none of that.

They had their coffee in travel mugs and a bag of snacks. Tim Calhoun kept checking for his wallet to make sure he had their cash, and he asked Vance twice if they needed gas.

"We filled it up yesterday, honey," she said with great patience. It wasn't the first time he had asked her. The old man's hands were shaking, but for some reason Langley had no fear about whether his father could make the trip. If there was one thing his father was going to do, it was bring his son home safely.

"Okay," said Tim but then just stood in the silence. This time of morning was especially dark, and the lights in the kitchen were insufficient to brighten either the space or the mood.

Vance, who was the most composed of the group, poked Tim gently on the shoulder to remind him that it was time to get moving. They were leaving a little early, but they had a few days on the road ahead.

Brian's wife and their kids were waiting in their rented house, as Brian was adamant about their not seeing him as he emerged from prison. He wanted to appear to them whole and in control, as was his way, so they were not going on the trip.

It had so far been a snowless winter. The weather had been variable, as it had been last year, with the wind blowing and short stretches of warm weather. As they all walked out to the car, Langley was glad to see the bright web of stars up above. There would be no snow today to slow them down before they picked Brian up or when they were bringing him back home.

Langley wondered if Brian would sit up front with his father on the way home, with Vance in the back, or if he would sit in the back like a little boy like they all did when they were kids. He wondered what the conversation would be like and what expression Brian would wear when they first saw each other. He had played this scene out in his mind a thousand times at this point, and there were always two versions.

In the first version Brian walked right past Langley. He didn't even acknowledge him. In the second version he dropped what he was holding in his hands and hugged

Langley hard and with a great deal of love.

Vance and the old man turned around in the driveway, and Langley and Delia watched as the headlights moved down the road and out of sight. They turned to each other and didn't say anything. Langley put his arm around Delia, and for some reason they did not drive back to their house but stayed in the kitchen of the Calhoun home. Langley made a fresh pot of coffee and brewed Delia some tea.

A car coming into the driveway startled them. Langley thought for a second that the old man just couldn't make it and had returned home, but it turned out to be the newspaper delivery person. They both heard the *Fenton Herald* make a light *thwap* as it hit the hard ground, and then the car drove off. It was just beginning to get light.

Langley went out to the driveway and picked up the paper, which was wrapped in two blue plastic bags. He pulled the paper out and unfolded it and saw the headline, "Brian Calhoun to Be Released Thanksgiving Day."

He didn't read the story. He handed the paper to Delia and turned to look out at the light coming up over his old back yard. He smiled wistfully because he could see and hear Brian's voice and his own and his brother Danny's, little Danny's voice which never broke, which never got to say or speak anything other than the things a child says or speaks.

"Jesus," said Langley quietly, putting his hand over his mouth and trying his best not to cry. He almost wished it would stay dark now. If it stayed dark it would mean time was standing still. That would mean Vance and his father wouldn't be traveling out west to the federal prison where his brother had been living—living?—for the past eighteen months, a place where he had never even been able to visit.

As tense as their relationship had been since Danny died, Brian and Langley had never gone this long without speaking or seeing each other. Even in the worst of times they saw each other on the holidays, and they had never let their personal disagreements get in the way of how they treated each other's children. That part of their lives was always good.

But now he wondered what Brian would look like and if his relationship with Brian's children could be rebuilt. Brian had not allowed their kids to see Langley, even though Langley had reached out to Brian's wife to see if there was something he should say.

Elaine said she would love for Langley to see the children, if only to explain what had happened, but she was also candid. "It would help if only to take their rage out on someone besides me," she said.

But Brian wouldn't allow it, and Elaine said she could not go against what Brian wanted.

Fifty-Seven

Thanksgiving Day, November 28, 9:00 a.m. Brian was home. The old man called Langley when they got back to the house, and he said Brian was tense and quiet, but he was with Elaine and the kids. He told Langley he and Vance were skipping Thanksgiving and going to sleep. They were both exhausted.

Langley didn't ask if Brian had said anything about meeting up with him. He figured that would just take its natural course, but he decided to read the letter that had been sent to him all those months ago.

He had no idea what it would say, but it made him feel like a little boy who was about to receive the worst news of his life. He remembered the nights when he had done something terrible, and his father's car pulled into the driveway. Langley would sit on his bed waiting for his father's angry voice. "Langley!" he'd hear and brace himself. That was what he was feeling now.

"I used to call you Barabbas." That was how it began.

For a couple of years after Danny's death, Langley had been Barabbas, the one who lived. "That's what a good Catholic upbringing will get you," Langley had said to his first wife Julia in bitterness when he first told her the story. "I used to call you Barabbas."

Langley's parents never knew of this epithet. Brian never said it in front of anyone else. He was always smart that way. Brian always knew what to say and when to say it, and that's why he was a good lawyer. Langley, of course, never said anything to anybody. He had been intimidated by Brian right up until the moment his older brother went to jail.

"I used to call you Barabbas."

Yes, you did, thought Langley, and he put the letter down on his desk for a moment and pinched the bridge of his nose. So what, and why are you bringing this up now? Langley was unsure what he was going to read next. He felt certainly it would be along the lines of, "And you deserved it," but that line of thought was the little boy in him who secretly held the blame of his brother's death so close to his heart that Langley had come to believe he was guilty of almost every trespass of which he was accused and many he wasn't.

Things were different now, and so when he read on the words came as a surprise, but they didn't hurt him like they would have before. Brian was saying that for the sake of his own mental health, he would not be able to see Langley again. Not ever.

I'm not sure I want you to, thought Langley.

"This is what they call a country club prison, but I don't know why anyone would call it that," wrote Brian. "We may be able to walk around, and I suppose the probability of physical abuse, including rape, is diminished, but still it is devastating, not only for me but of course for Elaine and the kids.

"The kids aren't able to make any distinction. Years from now they will tell stories about their father being in jail, and I can foresee the look of apprehension on their faces when we see each other face to face for the first time, the fear. That will hurt me for the rest of my life.

"Our father is a model of stoicism. He's been through many wars, of course, and I suppose I am grateful for his strength and perseverance as I am hopeful that one day his remaining sons may be able to give him some sense of equanimity and peace rather than the unending pain we seemed to cause so easily.

"I don't have much peace. I don't blame you for this, not really, but you are the only one on whom I will be able to take out my frustrations and anger. There is no one else. Not Dad, of course, and not my own family, and out of necessity any wrong that was done to me by associates or clients or friends I will have to ignore because they are the ones who will be able to help me back on my feet once I am released.

"And I will not turn my anger and resentment within. So that leaves you. It means your girlfriend. It means your children, both past and those that will come. It is you on whom I choose to take out my anger.

"I wish I could say I was sorry, but this is my salvation and, indeed, my choice. It's my life, and ultimately I can treat anyone in any manner I choose. So, brother, I am sorry I used to call you Barabbas. That was unconscionable, and I will tell you that I was fully aware of the kind of long-term damage that would cause.

"I am glad you are alive and finally starting to make something of your life, but that life will be separate from mine. I have asked Dad to stop asking me when or if we will reconcile. My answer is clear. We will not. Good luck."

Good luck, Langley thought. That's something you say to acquaintances when you bump into them in the supermarket, and they look like they're sick.

Delia took the piece of paper, looked at Langley and read it with an expression that began as exasperation and ended with a kind of sad resignation. They were sitting together on the couch in their house, and the day had faded into darkness.

Without saying anything she put the letter on the table in front of them. She sighed and looked at Langley. Then she picked it up and read it once more as Langley sat there. She put the letter down yet again. She leaned over and hugged Langley around his neck. "I think your brother did you a favor," she said.

Langley sighed and loosened his grip on her. "I don't know," he said.

Fifty-Eight

Thanksgiving Day, 4:30 p.m. The house was still filled with the aroma of turkey, and the day had been filled with all the details of every Thanksgiving he had ever known, but it didn't feel like a holiday. There was the meal, the parade, the football game, the wine, saying grace before dinner, but this was a quiet Thanksgiving. There were no voices in the house. No voices of his children, Nancy and Patty, or of Danny and Emily, his niece and nephew, not his father or his mother.

He heard the voices of him and his brothers when they were kids. They echoed. How happy they had been. They used to play a game of touch football every Thanksgiving down at the open field at the Burlingame Feed Company, but that was now a subdivision.

Langley looked at Delia, a month from her due date. It will be noisy around here again, he thought. She was lying on the couch, watching a Christmas movie. Langley grabbed a glass of wine and went out the front door and stood in front of the house. It was a mild, wet afternoon. He heard the voices of children, and someone was beeping a car horn. He sipped his wine and kind of chuckled to himself. The chuckle wasn't mirthful. It was a laugh meant to convey that he got it. He got the fact that the universe was absurd. He got it. Point made.

There was a haze over the neighborhood. The corridor of wet air that was just sitting on top of New England was warming an earth that should have been buried under snow. It had been a year of nostalgia and loss, and now he wondered about what he was about to change.

He could not deny there was something stirring ahead. The war with Brian that had once been far away now seemed closer. He could feel it moving in. He could feel the new baby moving in. He could feel that this thing with the town and the water and Lucy Williams was getting closer.

As Langley looked out on the low-hanging trees, their branches bare but wet and with bark soft as it should be in the spring, he thought he could hear, for the first time, the sound of distant gunfire. It startled him. His gently unsettled reverie bumped up into something more sinister. He thought he heard the sound of cannon getting closer and closer to him, and he took a step back toward his safe house.

Yes, he thought as he sipped his wine and looked at the darkening neighborhood, yes, the wars were getting closer. His relationship with his two children, with Julia, with his new love Delia, with his brother Brian and his father ... yes, all of that and more was happening and closing in around him.

Boom. Boom.

People were going to get hurt, Langley thought. He had been looking into things that were going to hurt some people. They were going to have to run away from the shrapnel. He might get hurt.

No, it wasn't safe anymore. The war, the guns and the danger had gotten closer.

Boom. Boom.

The mortality of his own new child.

Boom.

He was startled when he saw that storm clouds had pulled overhead. The clouds were massive, and they were billowing upward. They were the size and color of battleships, gray and imposing and bloated with malevolence, and there was a fleet of them sailing in over the trees. Their peaks disappeared into the dark haze far, far above him.

Then the rain came down, and Langley watched as it splashed against everything. The branches of the trees were swatted downward. The clouds overhead were low and black, and the thunder rolled and rumbled.

Boom. Boom.

The streaks of lightning splintered down from the clouds, as thick and jagged as anything Langley had ever seen. The wind picked up, the rain blasted sideways, the tree trunks cracked, and Langley watched as the storm crackled and blasted around him.

The night was so dark it felt as though the black vast tumult of the universe had finally curved to its edge and settled all its violence right there in front of him.

Fifty-Nine

Sunday, December 1, 9:00 a.m., Fenton, NH. Parks Kirstenwall headed up Fenton's Department of Public Works. He had been there for years. His father had held the same job, and his wife worked over at Town Hall in the Planning Department. Parks never met a government paycheck he didn't like. He was going to be one of those guys with hundreds of unused sick days and vacation days when he retired. Parks wouldn't retire though. The minute he was done working for the town, no doubt he'd go work for the state.

Langley had never had much use for him, but when Parks called and asked to meet him, he didn't hesitate. They met in the back employee parking lot of Town Hall. It was empty because it was Sunday. It was also cold.

Parks was looking around. Nervous. "Your friend there, the professor?"

"Dr. Schumann?"

"She's right."

"I know she's right, but god damn it, we can't prove it."

"In that contract did you notice what it said about the Dryhouse? That it's grandfathered in?"

"I saw that," said Langley. "I didn't pay much attention to it."

"It's not that they don't want to tear it down, it's that they can't," he said.

"Why not?"

"Jesus Christ, Langley, if anybody finds out who told you this."

"Parks, come on."

"There are old cisterns down there underneath where the buildings used to be, filled with coal tar, all kinds of shit, chemicals. It's how they used to store that crap way back when."

"What do you mean by cisterns?"

"Big holding tanks, thousands of gallons. Probably made of brick and concrete. Fuck the air rights, man. The blueprints to some of the mills down there were stored in the records department over at Town Hall until a few days ago, but they aren't there today."

"Who took them?"

"It doesn't matter. When you go to the town meeting, you bring it up. You tell Maria what you know about the cisterns. She knows all about them. Todd knows all about them. They're trying to sell the land before anybody finds out."

"That's why they're building the bridge."

"Lucy Williams put the fear of God in everybody. You need to tell everybody what you know."

"Why can't you tell them?"

"I'm not going to get fired now, man. I've got two years to go, and I'm done."

"How can I verify this?"

"I don't know, man. You might have to go over there and see for yourself."

"Go over where?"

"To the Dryhouse. Get inside it."

"You said the tanks are underground."

"One of the cisterns is timed to open when it fills up with coal tar from the river. It's been doing that for years. It fills up. It empties. It fills up."

"Right into the river?"

"Right into the river." He paused and looked around. "I felt bad about what happened to Lucy Williams. I used to see her out. I'd wave. I didn't want to go near her. She made me nervous. And I think of her sitting there in that fucking house of hers, you know, alone, and I feel bad about that." He looked off into the distance.

"I appreciate this, Parks."

"I just wish I had done something sooner."

He threw up his hands and turned away. He didn't say anything more.

Sixty

Wednesday, December 4, 10:00 a.m., York, Maine. Langley went into the kitchen of The Down East Inn, which was the name of Freddie Ouellette's restaurant. He'd walked through the main dining room and asked a waitress if Freddie was around, and she said he was probably in the kitchen.

Freddie was out back dressed in black rubber waders, and he was loading waxed boxes full of lobsters onto the back of one of his refrigerated trucks. Langley had seen Freddie do that since they were kids. The sight somehow made him feel happy, and Freddie, for all the wear and tear he had done to himself, still looked the same.

"Hey," he said, coming over and extending his hand. "How are you?"

"I'm all right," said Langley. The two of them spent the next few minutes loading the remaining boxes of the order. Then they looked at each other and laughed.

"You lost a little weight," said Freddie, tapping Langley's stomach.

"Nerves."

"How's Delia?"

Langley nodded to indicate she was okay.

"The old man?"

"He's good. Vance is good."

"I was gonna have a coldie. Do you want a coldie? Let's have a coldie." That was Freddie's word for a can of beer.

He didn't wait for Langley to answer before he reached into a cooler and brought out two dripping cans of Narragansett Beer. He pulled the top on one to open it and handed it to Langley, then he opened the other.

"Let's go smoke a cigarette," Freddie said.

The back of the restaurant faced the Atlantic Ocean, which on that day was almost a Mediterranean blue. The sky was filled with clouds, rows and rows of clouds, heaving upwards but with flat black bottoms. The tops of the billowy clouds were blindingly white, and in between them were patches of deep blue. The reflecting sunlight bouncing off the clouds made the day seem many times brighter than if it had been a cloudless day. Light seemed to come from everywhere.

Langley and Freddie put on their sunglasses. Freddie handed Langley a Marlboro. He took it, was rather grateful for it, and Freddie lit up them both.

Freddie turned to Langley with a glint in his eye and said, "I've been thinking. I think Todd's still pissed about the money."

Langley laughed out loud. He really laughed. Years and years ago Langley and Freddie had gone out on a Friday night to do some drinking, and they somehow ended up with Todd Philbrick. The thing that none of them will ever forget is they actually had a good time. They laughed all night, got drunk, and it seemed as though they would end up friends.

They all slept at Todd's house that night because his was the closest. After they got up the next morning, Freddie realized he had spent all his money. As they were drinking orange juice in the Philbricks' kitchen, Freddie turned to Todd and said he hated to bring it up, but could Todd pay back the twenty bucks he had borrowed from him and Langley the night before.

Now Langley knew this was not true. Todd hadn't borrowed any money. But Todd, who'd gotten drunk and blacked out, said, "Did I? Did I really?"

"No big deal," said Freddie, "but I'm going to take Chrissie out later, and I need that money." Freddie would later marry Chris, but they were only going together at the time.

"Jesus," Todd said. "Did I really? You, too?" he asked Langley.

"You kept buying people drinks," Langley told him, which was what Todd habitually did but hadn't done that night.

"Okay," Todd said, and he went into the next room and got money from his father and paid back Langley and Freddie the forty dollars he had never borrowed.

On the way home that day, their hangovers clearing up, Freddie and Langley had laughed and laughed. Todd later on figured out he'd been had, and his father later had some words with Langley and Freddie, so any prospect of friendship among the three ended right then and there.

Now they were quiet for a moment and then, without warning, Langley started to tell Freddie about Todd's contract, about what Chloe Brooke had said, and his conversation with the real estate guy. He told Freddie about Dr. Schumann and the conversation they'd had with Maria Tull. Then Langley stopped talking and looked at Freddie. He took off his glasses and started to say something.

"I was … I … " Langley was stammering.

"What?"

"I got it in my head that the river, this pollution, what Dr. Schumann told me, had something to do with, you know, with what's going on with our baby."

"Our baby?" Freddie said in a mock startled way that made Langley laugh again. But then they were quiet, and Freddie looked at Langley.

"Jesus Christ on a fucking cracker, buddy," Freddie said quietly but unhappily. He sighed, threw his cigarette butt onto the concrete and crushed it with his boot. He didn't say anything but went back into the restaurant and came out with two more beers. He patted Langley on the back.

"How are you? I mean, I asked you before, but how are you? Look at you, you're losing weight, your face is tense."

Langley lifted his eyebrows and grimaced. "Tired." He blinked. "I'm not sleeping."

"What is it you want to do?"

They were silent for a second.

"What you need to be doing is taking on fewer demons as you get older, not more," Freddie said. He tipped his head back and sucked down his beer.

"We need to do something," said Langley.

"Okay," said Freddie. He was always game for anything. "What?"

Langley finished his cigarette and flicked it out in front of him. He told Freddie what the real estate agent had said about the air rights and what Parks Kirstenwall had said, and what was in the emails between Todd and Lucy.

"Let's go pick up Dr. Schumann," said Langley.

Sixty-One

Same day, 6:30 p.m. "You boys have been drinking," Dr. Schumann said as she got into the back of the cab of Freddie's truck.

"Yes, yes we have," said Freddie.

"Just don't get us killed," she said, "or arrested."

Freddie handed her a beer. A few minutes later they were standing in front of the Oquossoc in the dark. The river was full, and the current was fast. They could see the moonlight glinting off the rushing water. They listened to the constant whoosh as it rolled over the rocks and out to the Piscataqua.

"When the current's like this, it's almost like a real river," said Freddie.

Langley looked down at the water and saw the small, swirling jetties of oil and the bits of foam—unnatural, unclean foam—and he looked at the side of the river where the old stone wall stood crumbling.

They fixed their eyes on the Dryhouse. Langley had never really noticed how dilapidated it was, how the bricks were breaking apart, how the small building was marked by graffiti and neglect and how the windows had long since been boarded up with pieces of now-warped plywood. There was a large orange X on the structure now. Its roof was blotted with years and years of seagull shit.

They walked over to the building. Langley put his hand up against the brick, just as you would put your hand on the belly of a pregnant woman. He listened, but all he heard was the river.

The three of them looked at each other. They walked around the building, around and around it. Freddie tried to pull on the old green door, but it was held shut by an ancient Yale padlock that was rusty but sturdy.

Langley knocked on the plywood, then noticed a small opening. They all pulled on it, and the wood peeled right off. The square piece of plywood dropped to the ground, and they looked into the hole. The sound of the river echoed inside the old building.

"Let me go in," said Dr. Schumann.

Langley helped to lift her up onto the ledge, and she sat, waiting for her eyes to adjust to the darkness, before dropping down onto the floor, which was now mostly dirt. Langley hopped up and went behind her.

"Be careful," said Freddie and handed Dr. Schumann a flashlight.

"You see any of Todd's people," Langley said. Freddie nodded, and Langley went into the Dryhouse.

The first floor was a series of small rooms connected by doors. The rooms were filled with junk, old clothes, liquor bottles, cigarette lighters and things like that. The building had a deep musty, moldy smell. There was a wooden stairway leading up to the second floor.

Langley pulled out his shirt and wrapped his shirttail around his hand and tried to open the door. It opened easily, if only about halfway, and Langley heard the sounds of the river and also the gentle echoing of dripping water.

"Ssshhh," said Dr. Schumann.

An odor was coming up from the river. They could smell something that reminded Langley of the chemicals used to develop photographs.

"Wait a second," said Dr. Schumann. One of the rooms had a sinkhole in the corner of the floor. Dr. Schumann walked over, crouched down and shined the flashlight down into the hole. There was a gap of about fifteen feet between the bottom of the floor and a curving brick wall below the building.

"See anything?"

"The top of the cistern," she said. She was lying on the filthy ground and sticking her head through the hole in the floor. Then she scrambled and stood up. "It's there, all right. God, it stinks." She scrambled up off the floor. "Let's get out of here."

They hopped out of the building, got into Freddie's truck and drove off.

"So they're there," said Langley.

"At least one of them is."

"Jesus Christ," said Freddie.

"Leaking into the river, into the water."

"Jesus Christ," repeated Freddie.

"What should we do?" said Langley.

"We'll let them know at the town meeting."

Sixty-Two

Wednesday, December 11, 6:30 p.m., Fenton Town Hall. The new Fenton Municipal Building had the squat, unfeeling look of an apartment building that might have been built in old Soviet Russia. There was almost nothing appealing or warm about it. The building had no style. It was all brick and rectangular windows, and it wasn't particularly inviting. It did not speak to municipal pride, and it didn't have the feel of a place where democracy would be protected.

Langley and Freddie walked into the building, moving through a small crowd of protestors standing out in front carrying signs that read, "Justice for Lucy Williams." It was a mildly cold, misty night.

Dr. Schumann and Chloe Brooke were already standing against the wall in the back of the Selectmen's chambers. People were filing in, and they nodded at Freddie and Langley politely, sometimes enthusiastically, and sometimes they glared. A guy named Jimmy Allen went up to Langley and pointed at him and said, "It's time for you to go."

Langley wanted to say "Go where?" but he didn't say anything. They were here to talk about air rights.

People were coming into the chamber in clusters, all ducking in from the cold. Freddie looked at Langley and smiled, and then he looked down at his feet. He said just the right thing to Langley. "God damn it, my asshole is on fire. I don't know if I have a hemorrhoid, but I can hardly stand up straight."

Langley laughed. He never knew if Freddie was telling the truth or just talking shit, but it was the right thing to say. When Freddie laughed his breathless laugh, Langley relaxed.

Todd Philbrick and his family came in. He had two beautiful kids and a great-looking wife. Todd had always been good with women. When they were young Todd had one joke that he used to start a conversation with girls. He'd manage to steer the conversation to the subject of dogs, and then he would say to a girl he had just met, "I have a boxer named Briefs." That was his joke. Some girls laughed, some didn't, but they all got the mistaken impression he was funny, even though that was the only passable joke Todd Philbrick ever told in his life.

The Philbricks threaded their way through the crowd, nodding at people, stopping to talk to others for a moment. Langley couldn't tell what Philbrick was thinking. His wife was clearly angry, though. Who knew what else was going on in that household? The kids definitely didn't look happy, but Langley knew that had more to do with their having to spend time at a town meeting than the fact that the discussion had to do with their father.

Town meetings are always noisy and crowded. It's an excuse to get out and see people as much as it is to discuss town business. Langley waved to his old high school friend, Amy Hargreaves, who was as pretty and animated as ever. He saw any number of people he had met and known over the years. A few he had even arrested. He waved to Antonio Meli, and he looked for old Ira Stuertz, but Ira was in his nineties now and didn't get out as much.

Langley felt uneasy about something, and he couldn't put his finger on it. But then he realized it was because Brian wasn't there. Langley couldn't remember a town meeting at which he hadn't seen Brian.

Britney Sawuko walked up to Todd with her notebook. They shook hands, and Britney asked Todd a question. He turned away, turned toward Langley, in fact. Langley looked right back at him. Then Philbrick looked away.

At that moment Langley felt someone near him and turned to see Todd Philbrick's father standing next to him.

"You're one of these people, spend their whole lives on the public tit, collecting a nice publicly funded pension, right?"

Langley just cocked his head.

"Do you go home after a day of destroying people and say to your wife—well, not your wife, your wife left you, but your pregnant girlfriend—do you say boy, that was a good day's work? Do you feel proud and fulfilled when you pop open the booze bottle at the end of the day?"

Langley didn't say anything.

"How are your children doing, Chief?" said Mr. Philbrick. He then looked at Dr. Schumann. "You'll certainly be hearing again from us." Then he looked at Chloe. He looked at her up and down. "Hello, beautiful," he said.

Chloe looked Mr. Philbrick up and down. "Hello, pretty," she said.

Sixty-Three

Same day, 7:00 p.m. "All stand for the Pledge of Allegiance," Maria Tull said. The audience stood, faced the flag and put their hands over their hearts, recited the pledge and then sat.

Maria then said. "As you know, we have scheduled this special public session with two items on the agenda, air rights and their relation to the property being developed on plats 1472 and 1477 in the town of Fenton, New Hampshire." There was a murmur, and Maria's voice went up in volume. "There will be no questions!" At that the meeting erupted, and Maria had to gavel everyone into being quiet.

"We're not going to talk about that, Maria. We're going to talk about the poison in the river." That was Freddie Ouellette.

"We're at peak capacity here. That means one hundred seventy-five people are in this room, all with something to say, all with questions to ask. We hope to anticipate your questions tonight with what we have to say."

"We're going to ask questions, Maria," someone yelled out.

"And we're not going to answer them," Maria shot back.

"We'll just keep calling your office, Eb, if you leave more questions than answers," the same voice said, at which there was some applause.

"Shut up," somebody else yelled. Eb Webb, the town attorney, looked unhappy. This is what can happen when people go into public service. They want things to go smoothly, and they secretly hope these kinds of conflicts never arise. All the appeal of public service goes away in the face of an angry mob.

Eb was taking some papers out of his valise as the crowd settled into their seats. There is always something thrilling, Langley thought, when a town comes together like this. He'd thought that even when they'd come together against him.

Eb was now holding a sheaf of papers. Maria banged her gavel, and the crowd quieted. "This is why we're here," she said. "The issue is a legal concept known as air rights, which are owned by the current deed holder of plats 1472 and 1477. We're going to listen to the town attorney, Mr. Webb, and then I am going to close the meeting."

"I thought this was a public meeting," someone shouted.

"This is a meeting of the Board of Selectmen. There was never anything said about public participation," Maria said.

Eb was a practiced politician, and what he did next was an old trick. He launched into a long preamble about the history of air rights, riparian rights, their basis in law, what their relevance was to the current construction property in town. He talked about the bidding process—and here he was much vaguer than when he was talking about air rights—and how the construction was split into different parts, which allowed the town not to have to put some aspects of the project out to bid, and how Todd Philbrick's company had the requisite experience to …

"Enough!" someone shouted, and it turned out to be Freddie Ouellette. "Enough, Eb. Enough, enough, enough, enough."

Maria banged the gavel.

"We're not going home until we hear what happened to Lucy Williams," Dr. Schumann yelled.

"You'll have to arrest us all," said Chloe, and there was more applause.

"There's poison underneath that land over there!" Dr Schumann yelled.

Maria banged the gavel again, and the crowd was silent. Eb Webb leaned over and spoke in her ear. Maria put her hand over the microphone, and Langley always thought that little gesture made the people doing it seem more important than they actually were. It was a gesture meant to convey that weighty issues were being discussed by important people, and the little people weren't supposed to hear. It was pure theater, even when it happened in Congress.

"We're going to ask you one more time. If you people don't say quiet, we'll ask the police department to vacate the premises," Maria said. "It's as simple as that."

"It's a cover-up," Dr. Schumann stated loudly, and she was shouted down. "The reason that land is undeveloped is because it's rotten!"

"Mr. Poston," Maria said, indicating the town manager, who was going to call in the police.

The crowd yelled "No, no!"

The town manager went out the back door and came in with a cop. The cop walked over to Dr. Schumann.

"You can take me out of this room, but I won't be silenced! Look under the Dryhouse! Look under that land!

It's toxic. It's killing you. It killed Lucy Williams!" There were boos and applause. The cop had Dr. Schumann by the elbow.

"Please," said the officer.

"Don't be afraid! Look into it." She was dragged out of the room. Someone else, a civilian, had grabbed Dr. Schumann's other elbow. "The land is poison! Your water is polluted! Don't be afraid." People were booing loudly now, drowning her out.

Dr. Schumann was still shouting as they took her out of the building.

Eb Webb then went into the history of when the public meetings on the contract were posted, how no one had showed up, how the contract was read out loud in public session and voted on.

Langley reviewed the minutes of those meetings, and the item on the agenda referring to Todd Philbrick's contract couldn't have been more vague or benign, but there was probably nothing illegal about that.

And then it was over. When he was walking out of the room, Langley looked at the oil paintings that lined the walls of the Chambers. He looked at all those stern, upright, sober men who had founded the great town of Fenton. They were in their white cotton shirts and their bow ties, and they all had that smug, New England Protestant, prosperous look on their faces.

He looked at the names of these men, the Ticknors, the Abbots, the Lyells, the Marshes and the Fullers. They were all captured in oil and respectability and framed in ornate wood, a context designed so you wouldn't question their motives or morals. They hung on the wall, as they did on the walls of public rooms all over the country, as some kind of affirmation of their greatness and influence.

These were the people that made Fenton what it is today, Langley thought. These were the people that made America what it is today. He didn't see a row of distinguished gentlemen. He saw a group of faces that belonged in a police lineup.

Some people thanked Langley and his friends, others didn't say anything, and still others glared. Chloe hugged Langley, another first, and shook Freddie's hand. Langley watched her get into her car and briefly wondered if she was going home to Mr. Computer Chip. He wondered where Dr. Schumann was. She might have been booked.

Freddie shrugged his shoulders. "We'll see what happens," he said. Langley walked with him to his truck. Freddie turned and looked at the truck parked next to his. The door read "Joe Wheeler and Sons, Stump Grinding."

"That fucking guy," said Freddie. "How do you make a living even grinding stumps when you're that dumb?" Langley smiled a rueful smile. Freddie unlocked his doors and looked over at him. "Good job," he said.

Langley shrugged his shoulders. "You said you wanted to look into this because you wanted a place for your kid to play," said Langley.

Freddie nodded his head. "Yeah, well," he said. "Not everything works out."

"I'll call you," said Langley.

"Call the minute that baby is born," said Freddie. "I'm looking forward to seeing Delia and meeting the father."

Langley shook his head and walked to his truck and went home. Delia laid her head on his lap, and he did something he had never done to any woman in his life. He sat there and stroked her hair.

Sixty-Four

Saturday, December 14, 10:00 a.m., Fenton, NH. Langley knew nothing was going to happen, and in a way he understood. They were going to develop that land sooner or later, jobs would be created, money would be made, and, sooner than later, Dr. Schumann would be forgotten. Lucy Williams would be forgotten. The whole episode would be forgotten. It was the way things were. Todd Philbrick's family would get richer.

The last episode was the ribbon cutting at the new bridge. The invited people were called celebrities but were actually the town manager, police chief, fire chief and chairman of the board of selectmen.

The absurd event was called "A Bridge to the Future." There would be a speech, the ribbon would be cut, and then there would be a small parade of the first official travelers over the bridge to the other side.

It was a gray day, industrial and gloomy, and the people who showed up were wrapped in scarves and jackets. Langley and Freddie were there, stamping their feet. Freddie didn't wear any gloves. He was used to the cold sea air.

There was a fire truck and a couple of police cars, and Langley waved to Chief Darrow, who nodded in return.

There was a small crowd of people on the bridge, including Todd and his family, even the kids. There were some other children about.

It was ten o'clock on a Saturday morning, and the whole proceeding seemed so small and unimportant. No one looked terribly happy. From a distance Langley saw Maria Tull give a speech. She read a proclamation from the Governor and handed it to Todd.

The ribbon was cut, and then the fire truck and the two police cars turned on their lights. Maria and the Philbricks and Chief Darrow got into the patrol cars and drove slowly over the bridge to the undeveloped lot, then turned around and came back over to the other side.

Langley and Freddie looked at each other and laughed out loud, but when Langley turned to look at Freddie, he saw Lucy Williams' house in the distance. He squinted to get a better look at the writing someone had spray painted on the front of the house. It said, "Fuck You, Fenton."

"Freddie ..." Langley said, and then the bomb went off.

Sixty-Five

Same day. Everybody screamed and scattered. Langley and Freddie fell to the ground. The cops started to yell for everyone to get back, to leave the scene. Parents were covering their children, their faces wrenched in horror. A ball of smoke billowed up over the bridge, and then everything was eerily quiet.

It wasn't much of a bomb, but it had punched a hole in the foundation of the Dryhouse. Concrete and brick had fallen into the riverbed. It was low tide, and a blackish, viscous ooze started to seep out into the shallow water. The cops were still yelling at everyone to stay off the bridge since no one knew if it had been damaged, and the fire truck swung around and started to hose down the Dryhouse.

It was all over in a half-hour, and eventually the fire chief, Fraser Lang, jumped down into the riverbed and walked over to the hole in the Dryhouse and pointed his flashlight into the darkness. He turned around and gave a thumbs up. Langley wondered how he could be so sure, but at any rate it turned out he was right.

Freddie looked at Langley. "Dr. Schumann?"

Langley grimaced. "I hope not," he said.

Sixty-Six

Monday, December 16, 1:30 p.m., Concord, NH. "Let there be no mistake. The event that brought to light the issues surrounding the toxic elements in the Oquossoc River was a despicable, heinous and cowardly act. We will not rest until the perpetrator of this act is brought to justice," said the Governor.

New Hampshire Governor Mark Ball was holding a press conference, and Langley and Freddie Ouellette were standing in the back of the room. They wanted to meet with the governor, but one of his staff said the governor didn't have the time.

"I bet he waited his whole career to say that line," said Freddie.

"But that does not mean we can ignore its implications," the governor said. He was calling for an independent assessment of the health of all the rivers in New Hampshire, many of which had mills alongside them, just as they had in Fenton. It was a big deal, and the governor was applauded for taking action, but Freddie said Langley should have been standing up there with the governor.

He wasn't, but that was fine with Langley. He had said to Delia a few nights earlier, when it was announced that the governor was going to make a statement on the bombing and what he intended to do about it, that he had mixed feelings about the explosion.

Delia had looked at him strangely. "Did you hear what you just said?" she asked him.

"What do you mean?"

"When was the last time you had any tolerance for someone doing something illegal?" she said.

"What does that mean?" he said, slightly offended.

Sixty-Seven

Wednesday, December 18, 9:00 a.m., Fenton, NH. The Oquossoc was dredged. They dug deep into the silt of the river and sucked as much of the toxic sludge out of the water as they could.

Among the many things they discovered in the silt were thousands of 19th century marbles, old glass of different sizes swirled with colors. They were later put on display and then sold off by the town to recover some money. No one knew where they might have come from.

The blueprints for the old mills were suddenly, unexpectedly found, and the approximate locations of the other cisterns were marked on the undeveloped property, which was now deemed to be worthless.

The town brought in engineers and consultants to discuss how best to discover what, if anything, was still below the soil.

One day a couple of weeks later, Langley went down to the river. For decades everyone in town had felt the river had been cleaned up. The time when no one swam in the river or ate the fish out of it seemed a long time ago, but now it was back.

He looked at the water at the time of day when the current appeared to be going in two directions. Langley wasn't sure if the tide was going in or out. There was red paint on the hard clay and a ring of orange traffic cones that marked where the tanks were below. He was thinking of

Dr. Schumann. She had left the area. Quit her job. Moved to Washington state. She had been questioned by the local police, the state police, the FBI and the Department of Homeland Security. She had taken a polygraph and passed. She had alibis for the days leading up to the blast and the day of the blast.

Langley, too, had been questioned, and so had Freddie. "I like you," Chief Darrow had said to Langley after their interview was finished, "but this is a whole new ballgame."

"You know if I had known anything about that, I never would have let it happen," Langley said.

"I don't know anything of the sort," said the chief. "I don't know anything. I've been fed so much bullshit by so many people, nothing surprises me, nothing changes the fact that I believe anybody is capable of anything today."

"That's too bad," said Langley. "So keep your file open. Do what you have to do."

"I'd keep my head down, if I were you."

Langley had shut the door halfway through that remark.

It was quiet around the river now. He realized he hadn't even thought about Christmas and what he would get the girls and Delia and his father and Vance. He didn't know if he would get Brian a gift or his nieces and nephews. He had no idea whether they'd be grateful or throw his gifts into the trash. He'd ask his old man to see what he thought. He'd say get them all a gift and not to worry about what they felt. Reaching out would be the right thing to do, he'd say, and he would be right.

It was cold, and he zipped up his jacket. He looked at the sky, which was opaque, murky. The profanity on Lucy Williams' house had been painted over a couple of times. The first time it was painted over, the message was repainted. When it was covered the second time, it didn't get changed again.

Langley had this idea that he wanted to talk to Lucy Williams in the way he'd always talked to his brother Danny. He had these conversations, and they seemed natural to him. He wanted to make sure she knew what had happened. He told her about how much she had helped them and what Dr. Schumann found out and all the rest.

"You should be pretty proud," he said out loud, and he grimaced, because these were the same kind of updates he gave to his brother Danny. After the business with the eagle, Langley had said to Danny, "I don't know if you'd be proud of me or not. I hope so, but I don't know. I did what I had to do."

He told Lucy Williams that he and Delia were going to have a baby. "I know you didn't have any children, but we'll tell our baby about you," said Langley, and he and Delia would do that many years later.

He stopped talking.

The sun was setting. The smooth white light of the late afternoon sun was hitting the tops of the houses. The chimneys and the peaks of roofs were bathed in the clear light while the first and second floors were already shrouded in early evening shadows. The sky was turning from blue to something less sure, a blue with gray or white mixed in, so the color was slightly less pure, and the sky looked a little less infinite.

Lucy Williams was gone.

Langley walked to the edge of the river. The sun was down. The river glittered in front of Langley now. The bright bulb of the moon threw out a cone of fluttering lights across the narrow surface of the bobbing water. Diamonds.

Ah, Lucy, Langley thought. Goddamn. I hope …

But he stopped. He picked up a stone—it wasn't even a stone, it was a chunk of old brick. He threw it into the river, and the diamonds, maddeningly out of reach anyway, scattered.

Sixty-Eight

Saturday, December 21, 7:30 a.m., Fenton, NH. Three days later Langley was sitting in Ruggerio's market reading the morning paper. There were continuing stories about the bomb. There were renderings of what kind of bomb it was, where it was planted, how it was blown up. They had to test the new bridge to see if it had been damaged. A couple of town residents were saying they were going to sue the town for pain and damages. Langley and Dr. Schumann were going to be deposed over and over again. One thing for sure was that the land, as things stood now, wasn't worth much.

Todd Philbrick came walking up and stood in front of him. "You and your friends killed it," Todd said.

Langley didn't say anything.

"What did you do it for?

Langley folded his paper.

"I played by the rules on this thing. You may not like it, but I played by the rules, and you caused a panic, and some people could have really gotten hurt."

He looked up at Todd.

"You've got a million things going on. Brian's out of jail, you're having a baby. You could actually do something for this town instead of fucking things up."

Langley still didn't say anything.

"Jesus Christ, Calhoun. What's the matter with you?"

Langley just looked at him.

"The whole town hates you."

"Maybe," Langley said. That much might have been true, but it didn't matter to him.

"You're friends with these people."

Langley had heard this before. It seemed to be a tack people took with him. Do anything you want, but don't ever do anything that might harm your friends, especially if you were doing the right thing for people you didn't know instead.

"Just … for God's sake, there was gonna be good jobs there." Philbrick looked straight at Langley. "It's still gonna happen, one way or the other."

"Maybe," said Langley. "Probably. Maybe not."

Todd sighed. "What do you have for me?"

Langley handed him the envelope. Todd gave Langley a condescending look as he opened it up and took out the papers.

"All your emails back and forth to Lucy Williams," said Langley.

Todd looked up at Langley and didn't say anything for a moment as he started to read, probably to see if they were actually his emails. Then, satisfied, he simply flipped through the pages and put the packet down.

"Did you really love her, Todd?"

"How did you get these?"

Langley kept silent. Todd read some more.

"So did you love her?"

Todd put the papers back into the envelope and dropped it on the table. He looked around and let out a long sigh, almost as though he was relieved.

"You told her often enough how you loved her, didn't you, Todd?"

He looked at Langley.

"I'm not talking about anything that's going to get you in trouble, Todd. It's over, but I want to know if you really loved her and made her feel loved. The law doesn't care, Todd. You didn't do anything against the law. I just want to know."

Todd didn't reply.

"But then the emails, the little love notes, they just stop. Boom. No more. I wonder why that is, Todd. I suspect it was just around the time word had spread just what a shithole that plot of land was, wasn't it, Todd?" Langley kept saying his name over and over, almost sneeringly, as a kind of accusation. Todd put his fingers back on the envelope but still didn't say anything. He sighed.

"Did she at least feel as though you loved her? Did you make her happy? I really want to know."

Todd almost imperceptibly shook his head as though he was trying to ward off unpleasant things in his mind. "That project, you know, was giving some people some good jobs, you know," he said. But his voice was soft, and he looked genuinely troubled. "And when they build out the lot, there's going to be a lot more good jobs. Construction jobs, retail jobs."

Langley looked up.

"Billy Cuddigan's worked on that bridge. He was out of work for two years. If that lot is built out he'll have work for the next five years."

"I know Billy Cuddigan," said Langley.

"There are people who depended on this work."

"I'm sorry about that," was all Langley said.

The lawsuits would come later.

Todd Philbrick, in particular, sued everybody. He was suing his father for selling him worthless land, even though he didn't pay anything for it. He was suing the Town of Fenton, he was suing his own attorney, and he was suing Eb Webb, the attorney for the Town of Fenton. He said he was going to sue Langley and Dr. Schumann, but that didn't stick.

The lawsuit against his own father was the most amusing. Todd accused his father of knowing what was below the land and deliberately dumping the land on him. No one came to the defense of Richard Philbrick.

It came out in the newspaper that the two Philbrick men had a fistfight. They were in the police log, but neither was in a hurry to press charges. Langley took no joy in their misfortune.

Maria Tull and Eb Webb would resign from their offices. Eb was accused of pushing through the municipal contract with Todd Philbrick in order to hasten the development of the land. He admitted he knew of the underground tanks but insisted he thought they were empty. It was worthless to try to figure out whether he was telling the truth.

Maria Tull simply said she had had enough of public life, but newspaper and TV reporters followed her for a couple of days, asking her if she'd known about the tanks below the land, and her answers were vague and unconvincing.

An air of discontent and anger rose up over The Shoals neighborhood, which was pinpricked with backyard wells, and every one of them was tested for contamination. The toxins found in Lucy Williams' well were found in others, so those homeowners, too, were going to sue the Town. It was a holy mess.

Langley wondered how many of those people hadn't listened to Lucy. He wondered how many of them were actually angry at themselves because they shut their doors in Lucy's face when she pleaded with them to listen to her story. Langley could picture them telling her to go away, telling her she was crazy, telling her there was nothing wrong with the water. You could still sense their fear, so their lawsuits were only a mask for their own failure to listen to the one person who actually knew what was going on.

He thought of Lucy Williams sitting in the Old Brown Tree that day last winter, and Langley remembered she hadn't touched her wine.

Sixty-Nine

Monday, December 23, 8:00 p.m., Tim Calhoun's house.
Tim Calhoun handed Langley and Freddie their coffee.
They seemed to have gathered as some sort of act of communion or commonality, but suddenly there did not seem much to say. They were sitting in the old house in which Langley grew up with his brothers. He had memories in this old house. His old man lived there now with his girlfriend Vance.

"I'll tell you who the real detested minority is now."

No one said anything. Delia cupped her tea in both hands. Her feet were up on a small, embroidered ottoman. She was days away from giving birth.

"You," and he pointed to his son, "and you." He pointed to Freddie. "Anyone who tries to stop anyone else from making money is the new pariah, the new outcast, the lowest of the low."

Vance put her arm around the old man.

"Mark my words for it. Don't try to stop people from making a buck, or people will kill you." He looked at Delia, who looked him back right in the eyes. Langley could tell she didn't like what his father was saying, but she knew he was telling the truth.

The old man then said, "At the end of the movie *Easy Rider*," and the small crowd made a joking groan. "Listen to me," said Tim. "At the end of the movie *Easy Rider*, Dennis Hopper and Peter Fonda say they blew it, remember? They sit around the campfire, and Dennis Hopper says, 'We made it, mister. We're rich. We're gonna retire to Florida.' And Peter Fonda says they blew it. We blew it. They screwed it up."

Freddie opened his mouth to say something, but he looked over at Langley. Langley knew he was going to make a joke but everyone could see the old man was serious, so Freddie just smiled and sipped his coffee.

"They screwed it up because they took the money over their own freedom, and it killed them. They could have just ridden the open road, gone about their business, but they chose the money, and so they blew it." The old man sat back and took a draught from his glass and shook his head. "We picked the wrong freedom. We all did. We chose pursuit of happiness, which now means acquiring the money to do what you want. We chose money, and we've given away almost every liberty we had. We should have just chosen liberty."

The old man screwed his face up, and then shook his head again. This was a guy, after all, who had gotten a letter from his government telling him he was going overseas to fight a war against Communism, who had the worst kind of memories a human being could have because he'd been told the freedom of his country depended on it.

Tim Calhoun never made any real money, but he took pleasure in the small things. Hunting in the woods by himself. Fishing. Spending time with his children.

Langley closed his eyes. His children. "Have you …?" He was going to ask his father if he had talked to Brian, but his voice choked up. Delia looked over at him. He cleared his throat. "Have you talked to Brian?"

"I have," said the old man but didn't say anything more.

Seventy

Saturday, January 4, 7:30 p.m., Langley and Delia's house.
On Sunday evening Delia said, "Langley," and because of
the tone of her voice, she didn't have to say anything more.
He went into the spare room of their house and got his
father.

"Dad, we gotta go," he said.

The old man and Vance had been sleeping over nights
since it had started snowing because he had that big Ram
pickup, so Tim Calhoun threw down his book and put on
his jacket and ran outside to warm up the truck.

Vance called Dr. Zolmian, and then she helped Delia
get dressed. Langley put the bags into the back of the cab
of the truck, and he and Vance helped Delia to her seat.
When Langley saw his father clearing off the last of the
snow off the windshield, a cigarette dangling from his
mouth, he thought the old man looked just as he had thirty
years ago. Langley and Vance sat in the back of the cab.

The roads were snow covered, icy, dangerous and dark.
It was snowing hard. Tim drove nice and steady, taking the
curves slowly and easing into a crawl when the lights
turned yellow. If no one was coming he went through the
red light to save time.

The ride to the hospital was about twenty-five minutes
on a good day. Langley was in agony, but when they pulled
into the emergency room entrance everything moved much
more quickly.

Langley grabbed a wheelchair, and Tim and Vance wheeled Delia into the elevator and up to the maternity ward. Langley checked her in. Langley called Ed Lustig, and said it was going to be any minute now.

"Take the day off tomorrow then, if you must," said Ed, and they both laughed, and he wished Langley well. "I'll see you in a bit."

Langley was about to tell Ed not to come to the hospital, that the driving was terrible, but Ed had hung up.
Delia was in the delivery room, and Langley waited outside. He told Delia he would be too nervous to stay with her, and she said that was okay.

In the hallway Langley called his ex-wife Julia and said the baby was coming, and Julia said for Delia to call her as soon as she could. He talked to the girls, who sounded vaguely, cautiously, excited.

"I'll send pictures as soon as I can," said Langley.

"Okay, hon … okay," said Julia. "Everything is going to be okay." She could tell Langley was stressed.

"I know," he said. "Thank you," he added.

He called Freddie Ouellette. He called Delia's friend Zemira. Then he sat down in a chair and waited.

Seventy-One

Sunday, January 5, 2:00 a.m., Piscataqua Regional Hospital. It was six hours later when Dr. Zolmian came out of the delivery room, and this time he had a wide smile on his face.

"Congratulations, Chief," he said, extending his hand.

Langley shook it. Dr. Zolmian patted Langley on the shoulder, and Langley and his father hugged like they had never hugged before, and the old man had tears in his eyes.

"Everything's fine, everything is fine," said the doctor. "Everybody's healthy. It was smooth, smooth. That baby wanted to come out."

"Can I go in?" Langley asked.

"Just give me one more minute," Zolmian said. "I'll be back." He patted Langley on the shoulder again and ambled down the hall.

A nurse came out of the delivery room a little later and told Langley he could go in. He went through the door and held it open for his father. Delia was sweaty, and the first thing Langley noticed was how small she looked. He had gotten so used to her being pregnant, it was a surprise now that she wasn't.

There in her arms was a small, wrapped baby. His eyes were lightly closed, his black hair was matted down, and his face, featuring the unmistakable stamp of Down Syndrome, was serene. He was breathing calmly.

"Honey," said Delia, "this is Jesse James Calhoun."

Langley closed his eyes and shook his head. He leaned over and kissed Delia, then stood back and looked at the two of them before kissing his boy on the forehead.

"My Jesse, Jesse, Jesse, Jesse," he said as he held the tiny little human being in his arms.

Vance and his old man went over to Delia and Jesse. They kissed her, and they kissed the baby, and Delia smiled a smile so serene that it almost broke Langley's heart.

He gazed at her, this person, this woman, this human being, this remarkable, mysterious creature. He was looking at Delia and saw a person of such power and myth and strength, a woman he relied on who was the one who'd said all those months ago that the two of them were going to see this through and have their baby and bring this child into the world. Only a woman, it seemed to Langley, could have that assurance and power.

And so it was. When he saw Jesse, it wasn't just as though his life had changed, the entire world had changed. Everything was different. His father was different, and there was nothing in the world that could tell him his own mother, Maureen Calhoun, wasn't in the room with them, witnessing this event.

"Your mother's smiling, don't worry," said Tim Calhoun just at that moment. Langley looked at his father, startled. He thought of those people, and he realized he would never again break up his own family if he could help it, never.

Langley heard a loud voice in the hall. He stuck his head out and saw Ed Lustig trying to give out cigars to the nurses who were working at the desk out in the hall.

"Sir, you cannot smoke that thing in the hospital," a nurse was saying, so Langley went back into the room. He held Jesse for a while, looking down at the face of his mystical little boy. Langley didn't want him to have any secrets. Secrets were too hurtful, too dangerous. No, he wanted Jesse's life to be an open book like Delia's, and he wanted the world to welcome him—not just welcome him but embrace him. It was going to be a hard world. Nothing about it was going to be easy, but at least they would be together, he thought.

Langley handed Jesse back to Delia. They soon fell asleep, and everything was calm and quiet. Ed Lustig was in the room now.

Langley looked at his watch. This was usually the dreary part of the night, the time when waitresses were putting chairs upside down on table tops, when bartenders were wiping down their bars, when cops were testing their lights and sirens before they went out on their nightly rounds. This was usually the loneliest part of the night, when the bands were putting away their instruments and when trouble usually started.

Langley went over to the window and put his hand up against the glass. His palm print fogged up, and he watched the snow come swirling down, down, blurring the parking lot below and everything around him. When he studied his reflection, he noticed he was looking more and more like his father.

The snow outside was so thick there was almost no light coming from the streetlights, and Langley watched as the flakes covered the cars below. He saw an old man, tilting toward the blowing snow, making his way across the parking lot. The old man had on an overcoat and a fedora, and he seemed to be holding something in his hands close to his chest, a package of some kind, something he seemed to be protecting from the cold.

Langley wondered where the old man was going and why he would be out in the snow at this time of the morning. He expected him to get in a car and drive off, but the man kept walking and walking until he went around the corner of the building. He had a feeling they were all alone now. There was no one else in the world except the people in that room.

The door opened behind him, and Freddie Ouellette came in. He went over and kissed the sleeping Delia, and he shook Tim Calhoun's hand, and he kissed Vance, and he kissed Langley. He didn't say anything. He came in like a quiet man.

A few minutes later the door opened again. Langley assumed it was the nurse, but when he heard his father say "Brian," Langley turned around and saw his brother for the first time in more than two years.

Brian was wearing a long coat and a hat. He was covered in snow, and his face was red from the wind. He had a bottle of champagne in his hands. He was the old man Langley had seen walking across the parking lot. Langley blinked his eyes as though he could shake off the vision, and then he clenched his jaw because he didn't want to cry.

Tim Calhoun stepped back a little to give the two brothers some space. Brian, who had always been taller than Langley, walked up to his little brother and hugged him, not too tightly but with affection and some amount of trust. Brian's coat was still cold, and the snowflakes had melted on the shoulders of his coat. When they broke from the hug, the brothers looked at each other.

Their father was sitting in the chair, smiling, and Vance

was in the corner, eating a cup of soup from the cafeteria, and she was smiling, too.

Langley and Brian stood facing the window, looking out at the parking lot below. The snow was coming down even stronger now. Inside the room it was warm, and the light was glowing dimly. Delia had asked the hospital staff to turn off the fluorescent lights overhead, and they had brought in table lamps. The room had the look and feel of a living room in a quiet house late at night.

Brian gently tapped Langley on the shoulder. That was all he did, just tapped him on the shoulder, and then Langley heard little Jesse gurgle, make a small sound, and he heard Delia say, "Jesse, Jesse, Jesse."

Langley was thinking of his mother, and he was thinking of Lucy Williams. Jesus God, he thought, and he wished they both were there. He remembered the day he and Lucy Williams had met at the Old Brown Tree, and she didn't drink her wine. Why didn't she drink her wine? Langley asked himself.

The snow was blowing fiercely, but there was no sound. Oh, Jesus, he wished his mother had gotten old. He wished Lucy Williams had gotten old. He wished Danny was there with them now. He wanted Delia to get old, old, old. And she would. They would make their way in the world.

Down the hallway Langley heard someone singing. There was a bell ringing somewhere. His phone buzzed in his pocket. Langley had put it on vibrate. He took it out of his pocket, and all it said was "private number." The only private number that had called him recently was Lucy Williams. She was the only one. Something fluttered in his stomach.

He pushed the button and put the phone to his ear. "Hello," was all he said. He didn't identify himself. He could feel the cold air coming through the hospital room window now. He walked a few steps toward the door with his head down and his voice quiet. "Hello," he said again.

"Hello?" a voice said. "Hello? Daddy?"

This was his daughter Patty calling. Langley looked to the ceiling and blinked his eyes.

"Daddy, is that you?"

Langley closed his eyes and drew in a deep, long breath. "Yes," he answered in barely a whisper. "Yes, honey, yes, yes."

"Oh, Daddy." Langley heard his daughter say that word through her tears, and there was nothing sad in the sound at all.

"Hello, my darling," he said.

Langley looked at Delia, and she looked at him. He pointed to the phone and said, "It's Patty." He watched his son, little Jesse, getting used to the warmth of his mother.

He listened to his daughter, and he thought how her voice sounded like her mother's voice and his voice.

Langley listened and watched the snow swirl down the quiet, dark street, billions of snowflakes carried off by the ancient northeast wind. Carried through the streets of Fenton. Carried over the old unhappy Oquossoc.

"Yes, he's very beautiful," said Langley.

"I can't wait to see him," said Patty, and Langley wanted to say she would see her brother soon.

"How are you?" he asked, and she told him, and Langley was lost in the sounds of memory and history and family. "I'll call you soon," he said finally, and Patty asked him to take pictures of Jesse on his phone and send them to her. He said goodbye and handed the phone to his father, who went out to the hallway to speak to his granddaughter. The room was quiet again.

Tiny flakes on their first and last journey were pushed and dragged through the jagged world on the thrust of the wind. The snowflakes were carried down the streets and across town and out over the bay. Langley imagined the flakes curling and dancing above the waves of the Atlantic one last time. He imagined them falling down and dissolving into the dark, choppy, white-capped surface of the sea. It suddenly seemed to him that not everything had to be measured by loss or absence.

Langley looked back at Brian, standing against the wall. He, Ed Lustig and Vance—beautiful, essential Vance—were talking to each other. Langley was only a few feet away, but he couldn't hear their words. Freddie was on the phone with Dr. Schumann.

Dad, Mom, my brother, Langley thought, his eyes closed. My brothers. The voice of his daughter on the phone. Delia, my love. My ... Jesse? Jesse. It didn't seem as though that word was a name. It was a feeling, a state of being, a universe.

He breathed deeply and saw his family in his mind's eye, people who were bruised and battered and all fucked up. Ah, Langley thought joyously, blissfully. My family. All of you. Thank you, my family. Thank you.

"Thank you, my darling," Delia said as though she had mysteriously heard his thoughts. And then Jesse opened his eyes, seeing his family, everyone who would love him for the rest of his life, for the very first time.

Meet Author Lars Trodson

Lars Trodson is a novelist, essayist and journalist. Currently the editor of *The Block Island Times*, he is also the author of *Eagles Fly Alone* (2011, Mainly Murder Press) and is the contributing editor and co-founder of the popular blog, Roundtablepictures.com.

Lars has been a contributor to *Cape Ann Magazine, The Andovers, Civil War Times Illustrated* and numerous other newspapers and periodicals throughout New England. He currently lives on Block Island, Rhode Island.

Preview of the first Langley Calhoun Mystery, available from Mainly Murder Press

Eagles Fly Alone
by Lars R. Trodson

One

Saturday, March 27, 7:00 a.m., Fenton, New Hampshire. Langley Calhoun hated death by violence. He had seen three people killed that way, and he truly hated each experience. One was a victim of road rage, another was the body of a young man who had his head split apart by a baseball bat during a pickup game, and the third—this happened when he was a child—was a situation so bad he never liked to talk about it.

A body that has been smashed open is just meat and bone, Langley thought. It is a sad thing because it looks like its mystery and soul have spilled out.

He was seeing these images in his head as he walked behind Antonio Meli, who said he wanted to show Langley a murder victim. Langley, the Chief of Police, knew he wasn't going to see the body of a person. But all the same, because of the cryptic way Antonio had described the situation, he wasn't looking forward to seeing the corpse, whatever it was.

It was warm even for early spring. The earth was wet after the thaw of the long, hard winter. The leaves and the pine needles, the twigs and the loam, had all loosened up into a thick mud. Their shoes sank into the ground and were covered in muck.

Antonio Meli was 82 years old. He was tall and thin—like the top rail of a New England fence, he always said—and his breath was steady. He was one of those Yankees born in the first half of the twentieth century that still trusted the rhythm of the seasons. He wore a light windbreaker, jeans, hiking boots and gloves. Langley was dressed in the casual business style he had adopted when not wearing his uniform, a pressed shirt and slacks. His shoes were all wrong.

They were walking on the back acre of Meli's seven-acre property. This back acre sloped up to the top of a hill and was bordered by a stone wall. On the other side of the wall was a landfill, and Antonio had told Langley earlier that he thought the owners of the landfill were connected to the bit of violence he had found on his property.

Every day for more than a year Antonio had been monitoring that landfill, which was a huge dusty pit that was filled up a bit more each day with the crushed parts of razed buildings. There were piles of bricks and concrete and God knows what else. The material was brought in by trucks that drove up, dumped their load and drove off, over and over, all day, every day except Sunday.

Just a few weeks ago something new happened. There was a flash flood, and a river of sludgy runoff poured down from the high piles of rubble in the landfill and onto Antonio's property.

Antonio took pictures of the hardened pools of sandy concrete, which was flecked with all kinds of debris and garbage, and he contacted the New Hampshire Office of Environmental Protection. Antonio sent repeated letters to the owner of the landfill in an effort to get the company to be a little more respectful, but they were never answered. Several attorneys had advised him to sue, but Antonio said anything was more palatable than going to court, so he simply pressed on by himself.

As they walked up the hill, Antonio told Langley he suspected the people who ran the landfill were now trying to frighten him. Antonio thought their conventional battle had turned into something more sinister. "They're a bunch of gangsters," Antonio said, "and I mean that literally." He stopped walking and spat out, "Goddamn it."

Langley came up behind him. He looked down and saw the decapitated body of a dead bird.

"Goddamn it," Antonio said again.

"Jesus, Antonio, it's a bird," said Langley.

"That bird has been killed, and someone put it on my property," said Antonio. "Those bastards are trying to send me a message."

Langley knelt down and looked at the animal without touching it. It stank. Its flesh was desiccated. The feathers were matted and broken. The head looked like a dirty, shrunken doll's head. The eyes were dried out but had a trace of fear in them left over from when it had been killed. The slice at the neck was clean, and there was almost no blood on the brown leaves beneath the body. Langley thought it was probably already dead when it had been decapitated.

"Those sons of bitches over there are trying to get cute with me again."

"I heard you," said Langley. He stood. The bird had gray feathers and bright yellow feet and long black talons. There was something strange about it. It didn't look like any bird that Langley had seen before. It looked like an eagle, but an exotic one.

Langley brought out his Blackberry and took pictures of the bird from several angles. He opened a small notebook and made a few notes. "How far are we from your property line," he asked Antonio.

"Maybe ten feet," he said.

"Do you see any other signs of violence? Any other dead or injured animals?"

"No, sir," said Antonio. Langley wrote it down.

"Anything else? Any knives, any kind of weapon, anything at all?"

"No, it was just this."

"How did you happen to come across the bird?"

"I come up here every day to check up on what those bastards are doing," Antonio said with a little more steel in his voice that usual. "You know that, Chief. I'm up here every day, checking my land, checking to make sure that my trees and ground aren't covered in some kind of toxic crap." His voice was raised.

"OK," said Langley. He picked up a stick and inserted the sharp end into the open neck of the bird. He lifted the head and put it in a plastic grocery bag that Antonio had brought along in his back pocket. Langley then jabbed the stick into the open hole of the body. As he brought the body up, Antonio reached over and quickly plucked two feathers off its wings.

Langley then dropped the carcass next to the head in the bag. Something about the sight of the lifeless bird lying in the bottom of a saggy plastic bag filled him with sadness.

"I want you to find out if any of those bastards at that goddamn landfill had anything to do with this," Antonio said, pointing over the stone wall. "They won't scare me."

"They haven't yet," said Langley. "How do you figure this has anything to do with you anyway, or them? It could be just kids."

"Nothing around here ever happens by accident."

Langley looked over the ridge into the landfill. It was relatively quiet for a Saturday morning. But Langley realized that the place had been taking in so much material for the past year that the piles of concrete and brick were now higher than the top of Antonio's hill. Less than a year ago Langley and Antonio had been in the same spot, and they had to look down into the pit. It was still a hole in the ground. But now the landfill, quite literally a hill of refuse, might possibly be the highest peak in all of Fenton.

A truck was unloading its fill. There were four workers on the scene. Two of them had stopped and were looking over at Langley and Antonio. One of them pulled a digital camera out of his pocket, pointed it at Langley and Antonio and took a picture.

"Come on," said Langley, "let's go."

Antonio tied the bag with the bird in it and handed it to Langley. They both walked down the hill and shook hands when they reached Langley's vehicle.

"What are you going to do next?"

"I guess I'll call the Great Bay Reserve and see if they know what kind of bird this is," said Langley.

"That bird is not from around here," said Antonio.

"And then I guess I'll call Bill Plano and ask him if he knows anything about it," said Langley. Bill Plano was the owner of the landfill.

Langley gently put the bag into his passenger seat. He wished he had a more dignified container to put it in. "Be careful," he said to Antonio after he started his car. "They're watching you."

"I'm watching *them*," said Antonio.

Langley left Antonio's house and hooked onto Goodwin Road to head back to the station. It looked like rain; it felt like rain. It had been raining since early February. The sky was gray and murky, and he recalled conversations he'd had in town with the few farmers that were left. "We need rain," they all said, "but not this much rain."

The *Fenton Herald* had run a headline that said the mosquitoes were going to be bad this summer and the plants would bloom early. But the mosquitoes were already big and fat, and there were blooms on the blueberry bushes. It was only March.

He drove down Goodwin and onto Depot, passing old Carl Deickmann's property. The house had burned down years ago with Carl inside. Langley went by Amsell's Farm. He saw Steve Amsell and a few other guys standing around Steve's old orange Kubota drinking beer. They were laughing about something.

He picked up his phone and pressed the number for Delia Reed, a forest ranger stationed at the Great Bay National Park.

"Great Bay," a voice said.

"Delia? It's Langley Calhoun."

"Langley Calhoun." There was a slight pause. "How are you doing? I haven't heard from you in ages."

"I know. I'm just … how are you?"

"I'm great. What's up?"

"Listen, ah, do you have a minute?"

"I sure do." Delia had a great voice. Langley loved her voice.

"I was called over to Antonio Meli's house this morning. Do you know Antonio?"

"No, sir."

"Well, he called me because he found a dead bird on his property. It was a … well, it's an eagle. I think it's an eagle."

"You're not sure?"

"Antonio says he's never seen one like it and neither have I."

"OK."

"It was obviously killed." *Murdered* didn't seem like quite the right word, even though that's what Antonio had called it.

"How do you know that?" Delia's voice sounded tense.

"Well, it looks like its head has been deliberately cut off."

"It wasn't in a fight with another animal?"

"The cut looks too clean. It doesn't have any scratches or lesions or anything else."

She let out a deep sigh.

"I have the bird with me, but … Look, if you're there I'd rather show it to you than keep talking about it over the phone."

"Bring it on over," she said and hung up.